Carson Kettle US Marshal

Carson Kettle United States Marshal
Book 2

by

Wyatt Cochrane

This book is a work of fiction. Names, characters, places, and incidents are products of the author's imagination or are used fictitiously. Any resemblance to actual events or persons, living or dead, is entirely coincidental.

© Copyright 2021 — Wyatt Cochrane

All rights reserved. Other than brief quotes included for the purposes of reviews, no part of this book may be reproduced by any means without prior written consent of the author.

DEDICATION

To all my family and friends doing the best
they can in these troubled times.

CONTENTS

1   Chapter 1   1

2   Chapter 2   10

3   Chapter 3   21

4   Chapter 4   26

5   Chapter 5   35

6   Chapter 6   42

7   Chapter 7   53

8   Chapter 8   61

9   Chapter 9   71

10   Chapter 10   80

11   Chapter 11   87

12   Chapter 12   94

13   Chapter 13   104

14   Chapter 14   113

15   Chapter 15   122

16   Chapter 16   132

17   Chapter 17   141

18   Chapter 18   150

Carson Kettle U.S. Marshal Book Two

19	Chapter 19	159
20	Chapter 20	168
21	Chapter 21	175
22	Chapter 22	181
23	Chapter 23	187
24	Chapter 24	194
	Afterward	198

CHAPTER One

Ice-cold rain poured from the brim of Carson Kettle's sodden hat and onto the brass tubes of the field glasses he held to his eyes. Between his breath fogging the small lenses and the raindrops streaming down the large ones, as much as he squinted, he couldn't get enough of a view to identify the men or even get an accurate count.

He could see that there were too many for them to capture without a good plan, and he could see at least thirty horses grazing not far from the men, along the north bank of the raging Red River. It had to be them.

The crest of the hill, where they wallowed on the sodden ground, was dotted with scrub oak and cedar, but the hillside below ran, grassy and clear of brush, all the way down the slope and across a wide meadow, to the men below.

Gilmour Bowean, the big man laying beside him in the red muck, bumped him with his elbow, and asked a question by turning his dark-skinned hands toward the sky and showing his pale palms, then cocking his head and holding up, first five fingers and then ten.

Too close to risk talking, but too far to see in the downpour, Carson shrugged his shoulders. There was just no way to tell. Why couldn't Bowean see that? Carson shook his head, then held up seven fingers and then eight.

Bowean jerked the field glasses from Carson's hands and snapped the leather strap against Carson's neck

Carson's chest tightened and his eyes narrowed, but he bit his tongue and held his peace. He tugged off his hat and flipped the strap over his head. Why did Bowean have to be like that?

Bowean slammed the glasses to his own eyes.

Carson pressed his lips together and breathed in through his nose. Bowean had started this outlaw hunting trip friendly enough. Why now did he answer every question with: "pay attention and see?" And why did he never want to stop and eat or get out of this freezing rain?

The one thing Carson could see was the yellow and orange flicker of the fire in front of a tarp lashed between two huge cypress trees. He could almost feel the heat coming from the flames and taste the bacon frying and smell the coffee the outlaws must have brewing. Instead, the pungent stink of his partner, and probably his own after too many days on the trail, filled his head and nothing filled his empty belly.

Bowean bumped him and handed back the field glasses, then motioned with his head back toward their horses, tied at the bottom of the hill.

Once back at his horse, Carson rubbed his stiff fingers under the sorrel's mane, drawing what little warmth he could find.

Bowean mounted and turned his horse west.

Carson followed.

After ten minutes, Bowean turned and said, "They ain't going nowhere tonight. We'll hole up and get back on them before first light."

Carson's shoulders relaxed and his mouth watered as he thought of the coffee and the beans and the cold biscuits, he had in his saddle bags.

Twenty minutes later, Bowean rode up a side hill, stopped on a small bench under a huge old oak tree, dismounted, and reached for the cinch on his saddle.

"We camping here?" Carson asked.

Bowean looked at him like he was addled and pulled the saddle from his big bay.

Carson unsaddled his sorrel and pulled a big semi-dry branch from beneath a nearby cypress.

Bowean looked up. "No fire."

"No fire? We're two miles away." Carson said as he broke the smaller twigs from the cypress branch and nested them together under the shelter of the oak.

Bowen strode over and kicked the twigs out into the rain. "Way the wind's blowing, it'll carry the smoke right to 'em."

Carson burned to re-gather the twigs, but instead, he flopped down against the oak and pulled a chunk of jerky from his saddlebag.

Once he'd eaten, he pulled the big, scoped Sharps from the boot under his right stirrup and wiped it down with an oily cloth, a routine he'd learned while hunting with his father.

"You any good with that?" Bowean asked.

Carson nodded.

Bowean watched for a minute more, then pulled the 12-gauge coach gun from his own saddle boot and did the same thing.

Once he'd finished with the Sharps, Carson did the same with his Winchester Yellowboy and his Colt.

Bowean did the same with his Winchester and pistol.

Sometime in the night, Bowean pushed Carson's shoulder with his boot. "You watch, now."

The rain had finally stopped, and the full moon lit the muddy world. Far below, the Red surged deep and dirty, and beyond, Texas stretched out to the south.

Far beyond the raging river, what looked to be a fire, twinkled orange. Maybe the rancher and his men coming to take back their horses and hang the men who stole them. It would be days before the Red was safe to cross, even if the ranchers rode west to Folsom's Ferry.

If all went well, Bowean and Carson would leave the cow ponies at Eagletown and have Jared Crusher and his men in chains and halfway back to Fort Smith, before that happened.

Carson crawled from his bedroll and hung it over a low limb to let the worst of the rain drip from the oilskin cover before he rolled it up. He shook his arms and stamped his feet.

Bowean cleared his throat and glared.

Carson shook his head, picked up his Winchester, and checked the horses, before wandering down the hill to where he could see the shallow valley below.

Why was he even out here? He could be warm in bed in Oak Bower, still dreaming before he got up to a good breakfast and started his day at the Fant's store. Even his parent's crowded cabin was better than this. Being a deputy had seemed so easy....

He watched and listened. Something rustled in the brush down the hill. His heart raced and he eased himself in behind the tree he leaned against.

An armadillo waddled out of the brush and rooted in the dirt with his long snout.

Carson sighed out his breath and scanned the area with his eyes and ears. Maybe being a deputy wasn't so bad. He just wished Bowean didn't hate him. He'd done fine on his own, bringing in Lijah Penne, when even Bowean couldn't find him. Why had Marshal Greer insisted he take this trip with the big black deputy? And what had he said before they left? "Gilmour can be peculiar, but there's none better to learn from. Just watch and listen and you'll be fine." Maybe that was the problem. The whole first day, he had peppered the big man with questions. There was just so much he wanted to know.

When the first tiny glow of light blotted the stars from the eastern horizon, Bowean rolled from his blankets, built a fire, and poured water from his canteen into their little coffee pot.

As much as he wanted that coffee, Carson was about to say, 'what about the horse thieves?' He hesitated, wet a finger, and held it up. The wind now blew from the south east. He glanced around the clearing. Trees and bushes would block any view of the fire except from directly south and anyone there would be on the wrong side of the raging Red River.

A few minutes later, Bowean handed him a cup of sweet-smelling, coffee. "Be quick. Even with the moon set, light as it is, those boys may move. As soon as we eat, we ride."

Carson blew over the surface of the coffee and sucked in an airy sip of the strong, bitter brew. Already, the day felt warmer. His shoulder's loosened, and he smiled at his own weakness.

An hour later, Carson counted eight men around the fire. He handed his field glasses to Bowean.

Bowean looked, then nodded back toward their horses.

Carson reached for the glasses, then pointed south. Twelve riders rode from the brush and onto the high bank of the Red. One of the riders raised a rifle and pointed it across the river toward the outlaws. A tall, heavyset man rode close and pushed the rifle barrel down.

One of the outlaws waved and the others laughed.

Bowean watched for a few seconds, then pushed back on his belly toward their horses.

Once down the hill, he spoke softly. "They're getting ready to move. Crusher's there, but there's too many for us to take 'em head on. Once we're sure which way they're headed, we'll circle ahead and find a spot where we can jump 'em."

Carson's heart thumped and his hands tingled at the mere thought of an ambush. He wondered if any of the others were wanted. They were bound to be. Crusher alone was worth $500. Today would be a good day.

Bowean kept them to low ground, and with no fear of stirring dust, galloped whenever the trees and the terrain allowed. Every twenty minutes or so, when they found a spot of high ground with enough cover to hide them, they checked on the progress of the outlaws and their herd of stolen Texas cow ponies.

About an hour in and close to a mile south, the

outlaws pushed the horses north at a trot. Bowean pointed northeast toward where the range of hills they followed, curved to a narrow, tree-lined band of grass leading through the hills. "We'll set up there. Pig said they take the horses to a buyer past the trading post at Ultima Thule and north of Rocky Comfort."

They sprinted down the hill, mounted, and galloped to a sheltered spot above the gap.

"Stay on your horse, but don't move from this gully until you hear me call out. Then move in behind them. Have your rifle in hand and ready."

Of course, he would have his rifle ready, and he wanted to say so, but he bit his lips together and nodded. His heart already raced, and his hands felt damp against the stock of his rifle.

Ten minutes later, horses splashed through the little, fast-running stream a hundred yards west of where he sat. He eased open the Winchester and glanced at the brass cartridge in the breech, then eased back the hammer and waited.

Though he couldn't see them, Carson heard the point riders and the first of the horses trot past. He eased the sorrel forward. Where was Bowean? The horses had to be almost through. Without thinking, he squeezed his horse ahead another step.

"U.S. Marshals!" Bowean shouted "Stop right there!"

Carson burst through the brush and found himself behind all the horses and the last outlaw, a tall man with long, gray hair. "U.S. Marshals! Y'all are surrounded."

"Heeyaw!" the outlaw shouted, as he raised his rifle, fired a shot ahead, and turned in the saddle, spotted Carson and snapped a shot his way.

Carson ducked and fired off a wild shot. By the time he levered in another round and found the front sight, the outlaws and horses had dropped out of sight. The gunfire stopped.

As the sound of galloping horses faded and it seemed sure none of the outlaws would come back his way, he crept the sorrel forward, rifle aimed and at his shoulder.

Over the rise, two bodies lay, unmoving, in the path. Gilmour Bowean stepped out of the trees, his rifle pointed. He rolled first one man and then the other over with his boot heel, then shook his head. "Ditch Kent and Bragger Bill." He spit. "Crusher got away. I had him dead to rights when one of them 'son's a' shot my horse. Lucky shot. I was behind that big tree. Almost nothing showing." He glanced over his shoulder.

Carson raised his reins and glanced east along the trail. "Should I go after them?"

Bowean shook his head.

Carson swung a leg over the back of the saddle. "You want my horse?"

Again, Bowean shook his head. "Check their pockets, see if there's anything worth keeping." He turned and marched toward his own downed horse.

Both men had bleeding holes right in the center of the chest. Carson dug through their pockets and found three double eagles and a wad of greenbacks. One outlaw had a heavy gold pocket watch.

Bowean limped a little, as he dragged over his saddle and tossed it near the bodies. "Anything?"

Carson reached out his hand and displayed what he had found.

Bowean took the money. "That'll buy me a new horse. You keep that watch."

"Are we going after them?"

Bowean shook his head. "No use. Help me get these two up on your horse. They're worth fifty apiece."

Once they had the bodies loaded and lashed over Carson's saddle, Bowean took the sorrel's reins and marched east. He glanced over his shoulder. "Bring my saddle."

Carson hoisted the heavy saddle and saddlebags onto his hip and hobbled along behind, slipping every other step in the wet clay. Why was the saddle his responsibility?

After a hundred yards, he stopped and found a way to tie off the cinch and latigo and balance the saddle on one shoulder. After another fifteen minutes, he switched to the other shoulder. Sweat dripped from the end of his nose as the sun warmed the wet ground.

What was he? A slave to a son of slaves? Why had he ever wanted to be a deputy US Marshal?

He dropped his head and plodded forward. One thing, the stolen cow ponies were easy to follow in the wet ground. As long as the rain stayed away.

CHAPTER Two

The sodden ground had dried enough in the warm breeze that, at least, the walking got easier the further they traveled. By the time they approached the Ultima Thule trading post, the full moon had risen and lit the trail. The whitewashed clapboard building glowed against a backdrop of dark pines. Despite Carson's initial fears, Bowean had carried his own saddle more than his share of the way, but Carson's shoulders and back still throbbed and his feet ached from the miles walking along the rough two-track road.

Bowean swung his saddle from his shoulder, eased it onto the road, and held up a hand to tell Carson to stay with the sorrel.

Why was it so hard for the big man to use words? There was no light coming from the trading post, so anyone there must be sleeping.

Bowean crept around back of the large main building. After a few minutes, he returned, and without a word, picked up his saddle, marched forward, and eased it down onto the porch of the dark trading post. He pulled his pistol, stepped to one side of the door frame, and pounded on the door once and then again.

"Hold your horses," a raspy voice shouted. "Who's out there?"

"Deputies Bowean and Kettle. You alone in there, Bridge?"

"Why yes, I am, Deputy Bowean. Those other fellers chose to gallop on."

"Open up."

After a moment, light streamed through the cracks, then the door opened. A short, fat, smirking man, of maybe fifty, waved them into the trading post.

Crudely painted red letters on a yellowing white sign showed as the door pulled into the light.

'No Niggers or Indians Inside'

Bowean brushed by the sign and past the fat man. "We'll have something to eat, and a bottle of whiskey."

"Heard you might be coming. Took you long enough to get here," Bridge said with a little chuckle.

"Never mind that," Bowean said. "Set yourself to getting us something to eat but bring the whiskey first."

Bridge's eyes narrowed as he bowed. "Anything else, Lord Bowean?"

"I'll be needing a horse in the morning, and we'll need a bed, but whiskey and food first."

Carson slid out a chair, but Bowean held out a hand.

Bridge set the bottle of whiskey on the table.

Bowean pulled the cork with his teeth, poured two healthy shots, and handed one to Carson, then tipped his back and turned toward Bridge, who stood watching. "Get to cooking," Bowean said.

Even in the lantern light, the fat man's lips tightened, and his face showed bright red. "Steak or ham and eggs?"

While the food cooked, Carson and Bowean stacked the two stiff bodies in the corner of the barn, one backed against the other, like spoons in a drawer, covered them with a dusty wool blanket they found hanging over a stall, then fed and brushed down the sorrel, before returning inside to their ham and eggs. Bowean wolfed down four eggs, a big slice of ham, and a mound of fried potatoes. "One more just like that."

When they had finished eating, he poured two more shots of whiskey. "We'll need two beds and more of this for breakfast."

Bridge held out his hand. "That'll be five dollars."

"We'll pay before we leave."

"I'd prefer you pay now."

Bowean pulled the wad of greenbacks Carson had found in the dead outlaw's pocket and peeled off five. "I'll need a receipt."

"I'll write it before you leave."

"I'll have it now."

Bridge bristled but wrote out the receipt and handed it to Carson. "Take the bigger cabin. The one with four bunks." He turned to Bowean. "You know where it is."

Carson sighed with relief as he plopped onto the straw-filled mattress, tugged off his boots, and fell back.

Bowean took a straight ladder-back chair from the corner and wedged it against the block of wood below the door latch, then he slid a bunk against the front wall under one of the only two windows. "Put yours under that one," he said, pointing to the other window.

After so many of his questions had gone unanswered, Carson just did as he was told.

Bowean unstrapped his bedroll and tucked it under the blankets of one of the remaining cots. "Tuck yours under that one and put your hat on the pillow."

When Bowean hung his gun belt from one post at the head of his bunk, Carson did the same.

*****

A slight scrape and rattle tickled and scratched at Carson's dream-filled sleep. He wanted to stay and tell Ange Fant how much he missed her, but a second rattle jerked her from him. He rolled onto his belly and looked toward the sound. Even in the dim light, he saw the door vibrate against the chair, then stop.

Bowean eased his pistol from his holster. Carson did the same.

Boom! Boom! Boom! Boom! Glass sprayed onto Carson as bullets plowed into the blankets and bedrolls on the bunks against the back wall, and one knocked his hat flying.

"Whooeee!" an excited man's voice said from outside. "That'll teach that sumbuck."

Bowean, pressed tight to the front wall, held the top of his pistol barrel to his lips.

"Best make sure," a different, high-pitched voice said.

"I know what I hit. You hear any stirring in there?"

"Just make sure. Besides, I wouldn't mind that

ivory handled shooter that big buck carries. Climb in there and open the door."

"You want it, you climb in."

Click! A pistol cocked.

"All right, Jared. I'm going."

A pistol barrel cleared the remaining glass from over Bowean's bunk.

Bowean stayed pressed against the wall with his pistol raised above his head.

First a hand and an arm holding a Colt pushed into the cabin and then a hat. When the rest of the head appeared, Bowean slammed the butt of his pistol down, threw his big arms around the outlaw's neck, and dragged him into the room. "Kill them others outside!"

Carson snapped a blind shot out the window, then hearing running feet, bounced up and looked.

Two men ran toward three horses tied near the trading post. Jared Crusher turned and fired, his bullet slamming into the window frame near Carson's head, driving him back inside.

Bowean's pistol cracked, and the taller outlaw slumped in his saddle, then tumbled from his horse. The smaller man, Jared Crusher, ducked low and, spurring wildly, disappeared around the front of the trading post.

"Truss this one up," Bowean, said as he kicked the chair from the door, flung it open, and sprinted to the back of the trading post, then disappeared around the corner.

The man on the floor groaned.

Carson pointed his pistol and held it pointed at the man while he dug manacles from Bowean's saddlebags with his left hand. He kneeled on the groaning man's neck and holstered, then pulled the outlaw's arms out, one at a time, and chained them together behind his back. He rolled the man face up.

The man's eyes fluttered open, and after a moment, focused on Carson. "Who the hell are you?"

"I'm Deputy U.S. Marshal Kettle, and I'll ask the questions, here. Who are you?"

"Jared's gonna kill you for this."

Carson laughed. "That's what Lijah Penne said, but it didn't work out for him."

"I know who you are, now. You're just a kid."

"And who are you?"

The man smiled. "That's for me to know."

Carson shrugged. "Bowean probably knows, but if he doesn't, those ranchers across the Red won't care. They'll just find a big oak and there'll be one less tick sucking on their blood."

"You can't do that. You're a United States marshal. I'm a wanted man. You gotta take me in."

"How do I know you're wanted? I don't even know your name."

"I'm Zeb. Zeb Crusher. I got paper on me. Last I saw, a hundred dollars."

"Jared's brother?"

The man shook his head. "Jared's my pa's brother's grandbaby."

Bowean's voice rang out from the back of the trading post. "You got him trussed, Carson?"

"I do. Says his name's Zeb Crusher. You all right?"

"Yup. Jared got away, but you got Zeke. He's laid out dead, and I got two horses."

Zeb Crusher sighed. "I told Jared we should keep going."

"Bridge," Bowean shouted. "It's all clear. You can come out."

Light streamed from the back door of the trading post and the fat trader stepped onto the back stoop. He puffed out his chest. "Y'all owe for those windows, and anything else shot up in there."

Bowean grabbed him by one ear and pressed his pistol against the man's temple. "You know about this?"

The smirk fled Bridge's face and shook his head. "I swear, I didn't."

"I find out you did, and you and me are gonna fandango." He pushed the trader away. "Get us some breakfast. There'll be no more sleeping, anyway."

"What about the windows?"

Bowean thrust a hand into his pocket and pulled out a handful of coins. He sorted out a half eagle and tossed it to Bridge. "Get to cooking."

Bridge spun on his heel and stomped into the trading post.

Carson and Bowean filled up on more ham, eggs, and coffee, while Zeb ate cold, dry biscuits. By the time they'd finished eating, the sun had crested the eastern horizon and light streamed through the window.

Bowean pushed back from the table. "I guess we'll need three horses."

Bridge smiled. "I've got some nice ones. I'll catch 'em up while you finish your coffee."

They finished the last of their coffee and walked outside. Bowean looked over the horses tied to the rail at the side of the building, eating oats and hay from the ground. "We'll just need pack horses. Nothing fancy."

Bridge's face dropped.

Bowean turned to Carson. "Put my saddle on that big dun."

"That's my horse," Zeb said.

"Not anymore," Bowean said, then he turned back to Carson. "Did you check his pockets again?"

Carson shook his head.

"No need," Zeb said. "I got nothing."

Bowean glared at Carson, then marched off toward the corral beyond the barn, with Bridge following like a puppy dog, eager for a treat.

Carson reached for Zeb's front pocket.

The outlaw stepped one leg back. "I told you. I ain't got nothing."

Carson grabbed the older man's shoulder. "You stand or I'll put you on your back."

Zeb dropped his head and stood still.

Carson pulled a folding knife from Zeb's right pocket. He opened the blade and tested it with his thumb. Razor sharp.

Zeb grinned. "Forgot I had that."

Carson choked back the urge to smash a fist into Zeb's stained teeth, as much for his own carelessness as for Zeb's lies. He bit back his anger and said, "Sit against that post."

Zeb stood smiling. "I don't feel a need to sit."

Carson grabbed Zeb's shoulder and kicked his feet from the ground.

Zeb's legs shot from under him, and he bounced on his seat on the hard ground with a whoomph and a burst of air.

"I said sit," Carson said. He turned and loosened the cinch on Zeb's saddle. Before he pulled it from the dun, he untied the saddle strings behind the cantle and tossed the bedroll on the ground. Then he dug through the closest saddlebag and pulled out a heavy leather pouch, covered in brindle bull hair.

"That don't belong to you," Zeb said.

Carson loosened the leather thong tying the pouch shut and dumped out twenty gold eagles. Unless someone came forward with a claim on this likely stolen money, this was going to be a profitable trip. Maybe being a deputy wasn't so bad. "Look what I found. Where'd you get this?"

Zeb pressed his lips together and turned his head away.

In the other saddle bag, Carson found a dirty Smith and Wesson .22 revolver. He pushed it into his belt, pulled out a pouch with jerky and biscuits, a greasy plate, cup, and fork and a couple of stinking dirty shirts.

Carson dug through the saddlebags on Zeke the dead outlaw's horse and pulled out another pouch with twenty gold eagles, a double-barreled Remington 95 derringer and a box of .41 rimfire cartridges to go with it. He stuffed this pouch of coins in one pocket, with the other pouch, and the little pistol and the ammunition into the other. From a compartment on one side of the right saddlebag, he pulled out a tintype of a pretty young woman with curls around her face. He turned it toward Zeb. "Who's this?"

Zeb glanced up. "Name's Bea. She be Jared's betrothed, and you and that buck over yonder killed her pap. Jared's gonna make him pay—you too. Let me go and I'll put in a word for you." He spit on the ground. "Not him, though."

*****

They loaded the three bodies onto sawbuck pack saddles and lashed them to the wooden cross members and under the bellies of the squatty little horses.

"That'll be three hundred for the horses and pack saddles," Bridges said. "I won't charge you for Zeb's breakfast."

Bowean smiled. "Two hundred and not a penny more, and I'll need a receipt."

Bridge wrung his hands. "I'd be losing money at that."

"I doubt it," Bowean said. "You can keep Zeb's saddle too. And those blankets and whatever else there is in that pile."

Zeb hung his head.

Carson pulled the little .22 from his belt and threw it onto the blankets. He had already taken the good oilskin tarps from the Crushers' bedrolls and used them to replace the ones that had been shot up. "You can have this too."

Bridge looked up. "Two fifty's as low as I can go."

Bowean mounted. "We won't even get two hundred for these nags in Fort Smith. Give him two and a quarter, Carson, and get a receipt."

For the first couple of miles, they followed the tracks left by the stolen horses. Already the air wrapped around them, damp, hot, and heavy like a barber's towel. Bowean pulled up. "These boys are headed southeast toward Rocky Comfort. I s'pose we best just take Zeb and these bodies up to Fort Smith."

Carson's head snapped around. "We'll lose the rest. Might take us weeks to find them again."

"Bird in hand," Bowean said. "'Sides, we're four hard days from Fort Smith. Imagine what these bodies'll smell like by the time we get there. Never mind adding more time."

Carson remembered the long, hard days spent finding Jared and his men. "How much are they worth?"

"Fifty each, last I looked. Could be some rewards out of Texas, too."

"Any local law that could verify for us and take friend Zeb here?" Carson asked.

"Maybe the Indian Agent back at Eagle Town, if he's there, but that's a day back."

Carson's eyes followed the hoofprints, cutting the soft red dirt of the road as far southeast as he could see. "Maybe we should just follow these tracks as far as Rocky Comfort. If we don't find them before, we could head north from there."

Bowean sat still a moment, then shrugged and turned his horse southeast toward the town of Rocky Comfort.

CHAPTER Three

Tom Green leaned back on the wooden chair. A fine sturdy chair he'd handcrafted from oak wood harvested from a tree he'd cleared from his own land. Their own land. Who'd have ever thought.

He held out his tin cup. With all the rain, the ground was too wet to work the fields. He had a little patching to do on the barn roof, but he'd already split the shingles from a good chunk of cypress heartwood. Once the sun rose over the hill and warmed things up, he'd get to it. "I'd best have a second cup, Sary."

He poured in a good splash of heavy cream, changing the steaming, black liquid from a color close to that of his own dark skin, to the smooth tan of Sary's. Then he stirred in a spoonful of the rich, sweet honey he'd dug from that bee tree. Even with smoke, the bees had made him pay with their stings, but when that sweetness hit his tongue, he forgot the burn of those stingers. He reached out, took hold of his wife's ample hip, pulled her close, and laid his face against her soft side. He breathed in her clean scent, mixed with the smell of the biscuits she was baking.

She scratched the black curly hair on his head and laughed when he slid his hand to her backside. "Stop that now, Tom Green. The children's still about."

He squeezed and released her. He had more than his share of worries, but today he would let all that go.

*****

Jared Crusher's horse's breathing came back to normal, and Jared's anger cooled from red hot to slow burn. Who did that darky think he was, killing Zeke and Ditch and Brag and maybe Zeb? By all that was right and good, he should go back and catch that buck and flay him. One day he would.

He rolled along at a lope behind the herd of good Texas cow ponies. Thirty-three head, even at a cheap fifty dollars a piece, came to a good chunk of money. If he lived careful, he could go a year on his share alone, especially now they were down to four. But of course, it wouldn't last.

Four men gone, good men, and two of them kin. He looked over his shoulder. Still no sign of the deputies.

He pulled his left Colt and checked the rounds, then did the same to his right one. He knew he'd reloaded them after shooting at the black deputy, but it helped him think to look at those little bits of death nestled in the pistols on his hips.

Who was he trying to fool? There was no way to outrun Bowean, and with more than thirty horses making tracks in the soft ground, there was no way to hide.

He pushed his tired horse up to each of his men and spelled out his plan. A couple of miles ahead, the road wound through a narrow gap between two hills. They'd give Bowean a taste of his own medicine.

He whistled, and they pushed the horses into a run. After a mile or so, his horse stumbled. He grabbed the horn. The horse scrambled and kept his feet. Heart pounding, Jared whistled again, and his men slowed the herd to an easy lope. Maybe the gap was further than he remembered. Zeke was the one always led the way, and now he was gone. What would he tell Bea? Somehow, he had to make sure she believed it wasn't his fault. He'd think of a way to pin it on Zeke and Zeb.

As they topped a small rise a neat farm appeared a half mile ahead along the road. Now he knew where they were. He remembered a big buck, about the size of Bowean, and his wench working the field when they'd come through on their way to get these horses. The buck had waved. Who did that boy think he was? There'd been a young'un there hanging out the wash too. Just the kind he liked: mostly grown but still all elbows and knees.

He laid his spurs to his horse, driving him past the herd, and led the horses into the yard. The horses smashed through the trellised beans in the garden and over the greens, before circling and dropping their heads into the little stream that ran through the yard, beyond the garden.

*****

Horse's thundered into the yard, and men shouted. Tom jumped to his feet, spilling his coffee all over the smooth oak planks of the table. He ran and peeked out the window. "Take the children and hide. I'll see what they want."

*****

Jared's heart swelled, and warmth filled him. There she was, coming out of the barn, carrying a pail of milk. She was flawless. Jared drove his horse toward her. She screamed, dropped the pail, splashing white milk over the red dirt, and sprinted toward the house.

His horse's shoulder drove her from her feet, and he leaped from the saddle and grabbed her as she tried to scramble away. Almost as tall as he was, she kicked and clawed and fought. Where was the big buck? There was no time. He slammed a fist into her perfect jaw, and her body went limp.

He grabbed her under the arms. He'd have to enjoy her later.

"No!" the big buck shouted as he ran across the yard, a shovel in hand.

Jared dropped the girl, drew his pistol, and shot the dark-skinned man in the chest.

"No!" a woman shouted as she burst through the door, a shotgun in hand.

Boom!

Burg's shot spun her, and Jared's drove her to the ground.

Burg shouted, "Leave that child. We need to get going. Bowean will be coming."

Jared hoisted the girl over his shoulder and flopped her over the front of his saddle. There was no way he was leaving her. "Gather the horses and let's skedaddle. We'll set up in the gap, like I said."

CHAPTER Four

Carson and Bowean followed the deep tracks in the red clay road, but with the three little packhorses, the best they could do was trot. There was no way they'd ever catch Jared Crusher and the others at this pace. Maybe Bowean was right. Maybe they should take Zeb and the bodies to Fort Smith, then come back. Crusher wouldn't stop robbing and killing. Or would he? A man could live a good while on what he'd get selling those Texas cow ponies. He could probably hole up for months, maybe even a year, somewhere they'd never find him.

They topped a rise and a little farm, the first they'd seen since leaving the trading post, sat beside a trickle of a stream meandering through a green field toward the Red. As they got close, Bowean touched his heels to the big dun and broke into a run.

Two bodies sprawled in the yard in front of the house, and it was clear from the tracks that Crusher and the cow ponies had been there. Bowean leaped from his horse and let the reins trail as he dropped to his knees and rolled a big black man onto his back. The pool of blood, dark red against the almost-orange dirt, told all. Bowean ran to the woman. She lay on her side, her head on her arm, almost as if she were sleeping with a shotgun near her hand.

Bowean touched her cheek, then stood and looked all around. "Why? Makes no sense."

Zeb laughed. "Looks like y'all got Jared in a mood. I 'spect y'all will be next."

Bowean spun toward the laughing man. "You think this is funny?"

Zeb looked at his saddle horn. "Waste of good stock, if you ask me."

Bowean's eyes blazed. "What did you say?"

"Nothing."

Bowean took a step toward Zeb, then spun and marched toward the house. "Check the barn. Let's see if there's anyone else about."

Carson stepped into the barn. A gentle milk cow looked up from her corn. As he climbed the well-worn ladder to the loft, he noticed the care, with which someone had built the little barn, and the tidiness. He remembered his father's farm in Oak Bower.

When he returned, Bowean sat on the step with his arm around a boy of maybe ten. The boy's eyes opened wide above his tear-stained cheeks, and he turned and moved back toward the house.

Bowean held on. "It's all right. That's my partner. He's going to help you."

Carson cocked his head. Me help him?

Bowean rubbed the boy's shoulder. "This is Tommy Green. Crusher and his men were here not long ago. He's got an aunt who lives south along that trail by the creek. You're going to take him there, then you're going to bury these good folks and take Zeb and his friends to Fort Smith. You can ride north from here and keep the hills always to your left and you won't miss it."

"No!" Carson said. "We'll take..."

"Crusher took his sister."

Zeb laughed. "Jared do like his young, dark meat."

Bowean leaped to his feet.

Zeb's smile fled, and he tried to kick his horse away, but Bowean snatched the lead rope and stopped the horse, then grabbed Zeb by the collar, jerked him forward and drove two mighty blows into the man's face. Red blood and yellow teeth sprayed.

Bowean pushed Zeb up enough that the bloodied, wobbling outlaw managed to stay in the saddle. Then he turned to Carson. His eyes narrow and furious, he said, "You do as I say. I'm going after the girl."

Bowean mounted the dun and spun toward the gate.

Tommy ran after him. "Please, don't leave me."

Carson ran after the boy and caught up before he reached the road. He wrapped the trembling, sobbing boy in his arms and pulled him close. "I promise I won't hurt you."

The boy nestled his face into Carson's shoulder. After a few minutes, his sobbing slowed.

Carson leaned back and caressed the boy's cheek. "I don't want to leave your folks like that. Do you think you could help me find a shovel so I can bury them before we take you to your aunt's house?"

Tommy nodded, pushed away, and ran to the barn.

Carson trotted into the house and pulled two well-worn quilts from the biggest bed and stepped back out.

Tommy knelt beside his mother.

Carson knelt beside the boy. "Let's cover them up."

Tommy nodded, and Carson spread the quilts over the bodies.

Tommy had brought two shovels and a well-worn pick from the barn.

Carson wanted Zeb to help dig, but the outlaw still swayed and fought to stay in the saddle, so he unlocked the chain hanging under the horse's belly, dragged the man to the ground, and chained him by his feet to a porch post.

Tommy chose a grassy knoll, not far from the creek for the graves.

Distant gunfire echoed, breaking the quiet of the day. Six shots. Carson stepped toward the sorrel, then he looked from Tommy to Zeb. What if Bowean was hurt? Or dead? What would happen to the girl then? He paused, then picked up a shovel. Bowean was the best. He would probably soon come riding into the yard with the girl. Even before they got the graves dug.

Once Carson had removed the sod, he took the pick and pried up the clay, first in one grave and then the other. He lost himself in the rhythm of the work. Tommy followed and scooped out the dirt. By the time Carson judged the graves deep enough, his entire body was soaked with sweat, and Tommy's hands were bloody.

They wrapped Tommy's parents in the quilts and laid them beside the graves. Carson jumped into first one hole, then the other, and eased each body in.

He climbed out and said, "What were their names?"

"Sary and Tom. Like me. I'm Tom junior."

"And what's your sister's name?"

Tommy looked at his feet. "Hannah."

Carson didn't know what words to say, but he'd attended church almost every Sunday growing up. Though he'd daydreamed through most of the sermons, he'd been to several funerals, so he closed his eyes and let the words flow. "Lord, we ask that you take Sary and Tom into your bosom and we pray you take this boy into your loving care and heal his heart. And grant your strength to Deputy Bowean, that he may exact your vengeance and bring this boy's sister Hannah home."

Carson picked up one shovel, and Tommy reached for the other. "Let me," Carson said, but Tommy plunged his shovel into the dirt.

When the graves were filled and mounded, Carson took the shovel from Tommy's hand and pulled the boy close. "Let's get you to your Aunt's house."

Carson mounted the sorrel and reached down and helped Tommy mount behind him.

"Hey," Zeb said, the word hissing through his broken lips and teeth. "What about me? You can't leave me here. I need water and I gotta go."

Carson unwrapped his canteen from the saddle horn and tossed it, then turned the sorrel south along the trail.

*****

Carson returned, riding past the mounds of red dirt. Still no sign of Bowean. He thought of his own sister, so young and full of life. What if Bowean was dead? What if Jared Crusher was riding free? How could he just let that happen? He couldn't, but what could he do?

He stepped around the puddle where Zeb had relieved himself in front of the step and kicked the snoring man. "Get up. We're going."

Zeb sputtered and snorted and opened his eyes. He scanned the yard. "Where's Bowean?"

Carson shook his head.

Zeb grinned, showing bloody gums where his front teeth had recently been. "Bet Jared got him. Bet there's flies buzzing his stinkin' carcass right now."

"Shut up!"

"The boys'll be coming back for me soon. You'd best let me go. I'll tell them Bowean did all the killing. You can just ride away. You can't fight them all."

Carson narrowed his eyes and looked up from tightening the cinch on the horse Zeb had been riding. He would be hard pressed. There were four outlaws left, and Jared Crusher was wanted for multiple killings. He needed a plan. But for now, he turned toward Zeb. "I said shut up. Now get on your feet and get on this horse."

After helping Zeb into the saddle and chaining his ankles together under the animal's belly, he mounted his own horse, picked up the lead rope and headed toward the road. Zeb's horse and three pack horses, tied head to tail, followed.

A mile further along the road, they approached a long ridge of high ground. The trail swooped straight south and then east through a tree-lined gap in the hills.

Something caught Carson's eye, and he glanced

down. An empty brass shell casing lay in the dirt. Further on, he spotted another. Pushing the sorrel into a clump of brush, he scanned the scattered pine trees on the hillsides on either side of the gap. He glanced at the horses for signs they saw or smelled something he didn't, but they all stood, floppy-eared, swatting at flies. He pulled out his field glasses and again scanned the hills on either side of the road.

"Look for buzzards," Zeb said.

"What?"

"That's how you'll find your partner."

"You don't want to lose more teeth; you'll keep your lips closed."

"Just saying."

"Closed."

They stayed on the road and entered the gap in the hills.

"Look there," Zeb said.

"I said be quiet," Carson said, yet his eyes followed the direction Zeb pointed with his gnarly finger and found a splash of blood on a flat rock.

"I told you."

Carson's chest tightened. "Doesn't mean anything. Could be a horse or Jared or one of his men."

"Watch for buzzards."

They continued along the road, finding more and more blood.

As they rounded a bend and broke from the hills, Bowean slumped against the big dun, his left arm clutching the saddle horn, his forehead against the seat, and the reins trailing from the bit to the ground. Clotted blood hung like red icicles from the tips of the fingers of his right hand.

"What'd I tell ya," Zeb said.

Bowean jerked alert and found them with bleary eyes. His right shoulder moved as if he were going for his pistol, but his lower arm swung as if on a string. His face tightened and his eyes narrowed with pain, then lit with recognition. "Carson. They're getting away. We've got to help that girl."

Carson rode close and leaped from the saddle. "We've got to fix that arm first."

Bowean's eyes focused. He glanced down at his right arm and nodded. "Hurry."

Carson helped the big deputy sit, then tore strips from a clean shirt he pulled from his saddlebags and bound them around the big man's arm.

Bowean winced as Carson knotted the last bandage. "Help me back up. We've wasted enough time. Too much."

Carson stepped back. "You'll sure lose that arm if we don't get you to a doctor."

Bowean slowly looked at his bandaged arm and then at Carson. He nodded his head. "The postmaster at Rocky Comfort was a medic during the war. Folks say he's better than any doctor in the country."

Carson used the rest of the shirt to bind Bowean's arm against his body, then he wrapped his arms around Bowean's waist and hoisted while the big man mounted.

"He's done for," Zeb said. "Best let me go."

Carson pulled his Colt. "Dead or alive. You chose."

"Just trying to help."

Carson cocked the pistol, and Zeb shut his mouth.

As they rode, Bowean slouched deeper and deeper in the saddle, until Carson feared he might fall off. "Stay with us, Bowean," Carson said.

"I'm all right," Bowean said.

The big man's dark skin now shone gray under a sheen of sweat, and flies swarmed and buzzed around his bloody sleeve and hand. Carson didn't know much about wounds, but he doubted even the best surgeon could save Bowean's bullet-shattered arm, let alone a former army medic. Maybe it wasn't as bad as it looked. Maybe Bowean could still ride once the postmaster fixed him up. Carson sagged in the saddle. There was no way.

Jared Crusher had Hannah, and someone had to bring her back.

Carson shivered. That someone was Carson Kettle.

CHAPTER Five

Jared, riding in front of the cow ponies, held them to a hellish pace. The girl, now awake, sat in front of him on the saddle, his right arm tight around her body. He dropped his nose into her curly hair and breathed in. Fear, mixed with her sweet scent, sent shivers up and down his back.

She'd awakened screaming, but a few good hammer fists to her back had stopped that. Now as he squeezed her close, her pounding heart and gentle sobs filled him with anticipation.

He glanced over his shoulder. Their horses' ears bouncing with fatigue, Burg, Ankor, and Willy, grim-faced and resolute, whipped their mounts with the tails of their reins and pushed the cow ponies along the road behind him. They'd likely have to shoot these saddle horses and take four of the best cow ponies, but for now, he dug his spurs into his horses' sides and kept him running.

The big buck deputy was dead. He'd shot him himself, but there'd been two of those U.S. blood suckers back at the trading post. Him and the boys could set up another ambush... He pressed his nose to the baby wench's kinky hair and his entire body came alive, even more alive than when his bullet had knocked United States Marshall Gilmour Bowean from his saddle. They'd be best to get rid of the horses and split up.

As they approached the village of Rocky Comfort, Burg whistled and waved his arm toward the south.

Jared thought a moment, then shook his head, whooped, and grinned as he led them right down the main street, past the store and the saloon and the post office. Joy coursed up and down his spine. He'd never felt freer. He'd be a hero now, to those that mattered. The hombre that killed the great Gilmour Bowean, and it didn't matter what else he ever did. There was only one outcome if they caught him. They could only hang him once. Today was his lucky day. He'd be a legend now, and they'd never catch him. Not down here in lower Arkansas. This was his ground.

He, once again, pressed his nose to the girl's head. She smelled a little of the cow she'd milked, but beneath that, only fear and sweetness.

A mile east, he led the cow ponies north along a two-track trail. He lifted his legs and jabbed his spurs into the big bay's sides. The horse barely responded. Good thing they were almost there.

Two miles north, he turned and led the herd under an arched gate of thick pine trunks, and down the road toward a big, round, pine-pole corral that stood beyond a log barn and a log cabin. The gate to the corral stood open. It was a lucky day. He skirted the gate and let the cow ponies stream by and into the corral.

Willy jumped down and dragged the heavy gate closed. Wild-eyed, the cow ponies circled once, then skidded to a stop and skittered, as one, like a flock of blackbirds, back the other way and stopped again, their sides heaving and nostrils flared and bright red.

A slight old man limped out of the house, long strands of sparse hair flapping around his mostly bald head, and a double-barrel bird gun in hand. He glanced at the road, then back at Jared, then back at the road. "Who's chasing you? Open that gate and get on out of here."

Jared smiled and stepped down. "Ankor, hold on to this girl. You other two, catch us out four of those cow ponies, while I get paid."

"You ain't getting nothing," the old man said, glancing over his shoulder.

"Fifty a head, Uncle," Jared said. "And cheap at that."

"Ain't nothing cheap when a man's hanging from a rope. Who's after you? Ranchers or the law?"

Jared grinned. "What makes you say that, Uncle Herschel? We's just in a hurry."

The old man swung the shotgun past each of the men. "Hurry on down the road. I ain't buying no horses today. Not like this."

Jared smiled even bigger. This was going to be fun. He held his hands, palms up, and away from his pistols as he stepped toward the old man. "What's this? We had a deal."

"Look at your horses."

Jared glanced at his own bay's bleeding, heaving, spur-ripped sides. "Like I said, we's just in a hurry." He opened his eyes wide and looked past the old man and down the road. "Oh, look there!"

The old man glanced over his shoulder. Jared stepped in, threw an arm over the shotgun, twisted it from the old man's grasp, and swung it by the barrel.

The walnut gunstock cracked against the side of the old man's head, driving him to the ground. By the time his old blue eyes stopped fluttering and came back into focus, Jared had pulled the brass-hulled shotgun shells from the twin barrels, tossed the shotgun into the dirt, and pointed his pistol.

"We ain't got time to dawdle and eat lunch today, so just pick yourself up and fetch our money, and we'll be on our way."

Herschel pushed himself to his feet and wobbled toward the house. As they passed the barn, Jared shouted, "Aunt Agnes. I'm coming in with Uncle Herschel. I've got my pistol pressed agin his ribs. You come on out, and I best see the palms of your wrinkly old hands."

"Do as he says, Agnes," Herschel shouted. "He's a damn fool, but he ain't fooling."

A bent old woman with long, white hair, hanging past over her cheeks and past her shoulders, hobbled out the door and turned her arthritic claws until the palms faced out. She spit a stream of brown tobacco juice onto the ground. "Why you doing this, Jared Crusher? Why you bringing us this grief, and me your ma's sister."

Jared smiled. "No offense, meant, Aunt. We're just in a bit of a hurry today."

"Whoever's trailing you will track those horse's right here," she said.

"Then you best fetch my money and get to hiding those ponies. I figure fifteen hundred for the lot. Thirty or so good Texas ponies."

She spit again. "We'll give you seven for the trouble, and not a penny more."

Jared hesitated. "Count it out. And no funny stuff."

Agnes glanced south along the road. "How far back are they?"

Jared grinned. "Haven't seen them. Might not even be coming. They've got some burying to do," he said, with a wink.

The old woman frowned and turned back into the house. Coins clinked and rattled on a wooden table.

She came out and extended a leather pouch, heavy with gold coins.

"Bring it down here and count it out."

Jared motioned with his fingers. "Never mind. I guess I'll trust you. Just bring it here."

She hobbled off the porch and extended the pouch.

Jared grabbed her loose-skinned wrist and slammed his pistol down onto the top of his uncle's head, then backhanded his aunt and drove her to the ground. As she rolled over and pushed up to her knees, he shoved her back to the ground with his foot. "Stay down."

He ran into the house and scooped all the remaining gold coins from the table into the pouch.

As he stepped back onto the porch, Ankor shouted, "Want me to saddle a pony for the girl?"

"No, she can ride with me."

Warmth flooded him. It was a good day.

His aunt sat with his uncle's bloody head in her lap. She looked up and shook her head.

He pulled a small handful of gold coins from the pouch and tossed them into the dirt near her knees.

She was blood kin, after all "I'll give your best to my ma."

He grabbed the girl under the arms and bent his legs to lift her into his saddle. Her legs gave way and her body fell limp. He grunted and tried to swing her onto the stocky gray cow pony. Her legs flopped forward, and the pony skittered off to the end of his reins. "You get up there," he said, as he again swung her limp body toward the pony.

He pinched her arm as hard as he could. She stiffened for a second, then fell limp again. He threw her to the ground and stepped toward his new pony. If the fight had already left her, what good was she? He paused; his bright, sunny mood all gone. Maybe once she was rested, her spirit would come back. If not, he'd give her to the boys. "Willy, jump down here and lift her up to me."

He circled the nervous pony and looked south. Still no sign of pursuit. "Burg. Open the gate and booger them ponies out."

Burg cocked his head and looked at him.

Jared pointed to his aunt and uncle still on the ground. "They're kin. Be best if they ain't in that corral if any deputies come."

He rode by his aunt as they left. "You can gather those ponies once the deputies are gone. Tell 'em we robbed you and skedaddled."

"You did," she said. She spit a stream of tobacco juice on his pony's white foreleg. "What are you doing with that child?"

"She's no child. She's half grown, and she's an orphan," he said with a girlish giggle.

"What's your name, child?" the old woman asked.

The girl raised her head. "Hannah, ma'am."

The old woman shook a gnarled finger at her nephew. "You leave her here with me."

The girl stiffened and leaned toward the old woman.

Jared laughed. "You'd just turn her into a field hand." He stroked the girl's hair. "Me and this picaninny got bigger plans than that, don't we sweet Miss Hannah." He smiled and tipped his hat. "Been nice seeing you two."

The girl slumped, and it was all he could do to hold her as he led his men north. He smiled. This was his country. No deputy in his right mind would follow him into these hills.

CHAPTER Six

The chain between old Zeb's feet rattled as they trotted to the edge of the town of Rocky Comfort. Approaching the town, the tracks they followed disappeared in the tangle of deep ruts, hoofprints, and puddles in the mucky, busy road. Carson shook his head. It didn't make sense. Jared and his men had driven the horses right through town. Why weren't they more afraid?

Bowean's head bounced in time to his horse, but his eyes scanned the street ahead and the boardwalks fronting the businesses on either side.

Wagons and horses and people tiptoeing through the mud forced Carson to slow the horses to a walk. People stopped and stared and pointed as they rode past. Carson pulled back his jacket to show the badge on his chest.

He tied Zeb's horse and his own to the hitching rail and bounded into the post office.

Postmaster Wallace stepped onto the wide, smooth planked, covered porch, and before he even closed the door, said, "hep me get him down."

Zeb laughed. "Don't wanna help that buck, Wallace. Jared's the one shot him. He won't look kind if you save the boy."

Carson glared, and Zeb closed his lips but held a surly smirk on his face.

Bowean swung his leg over the saddle, then his left leg gave out and he fell into Carson's and Wallace's arms. His dark eyes squeezed shut, but he held his tongue.

Carson ducked under the big man's left arm and acted as a crutch, helping Bowean climb the two wooden stairs and stumble across the wide porch and into the post office.

"Take him through there," Wallace said, pointing to a door beside the long, polished counter and the mail slots along the back wall. He closed and locked the door behind them and turned the closed sign out.

Carson helped Bowean sit on a metal cot covered with a gray wool blanket, the corners tucked tightly, just as his father did them.

Bowean looked up and met Carson's eyes as if seeing them for the first time. "Where's the girl? ...Crusher's got her." He pushed up as if to rise.

Wallace pressed on his left shoulder and held him down. "You're in no condition to go anywhere, suh."

Bowean grabbed Carson's wrist. "You go on, Carson. You can do it. They took that boy's sister."

Carson glanced at Wallace. "Do you need my help?"

Wallace looked at Bowean. "Do I need his help?"

Bowean shook his head and looked at Carson. "Go!"

"Is there a sheriff and a jail here?" Carson asked.

Wallace nodded. "Yes, suh. Little further along the street."

"Undertaker?"

Wallace kept his eyes on the bloody bandages he unwrapped from Bowean's upper arm. "Little futher down, yet."

"I'll see if the sheriff will take Zeb. I'll stop back before I go." As he stepped from the back room into the main counter area of the post office, a crowd had begun to gather outside around Zeb.

Zeb sat up and addressed the crowd. "You boys all know me, and you know these good men hanging over these saddles. You gonna let some wet-behind-the-ears deputy from Fort Smith take me?"

Carson froze.

"Jared won't look on it kindly, and you all know how he can be."

Carson slid out his Colt, inched back the bolt on the door, and walked through. "Step back. I'm United States Deputy Marshal Kettle, and this man's my prisoner."

"Don't listen to him," Zeb said. "Y'all know me. Y'all know my family. He can't do nothin' if you all rush him at once.

Carson waved the pistol and eased toward Bowean's horse."

"Gill," Zeb said. "Lead the way."

Carson pointed his Colt at Zeb's belly. "Shut up!"

A squat man with a purple birthmark covering the upper half of his face, stepped forward and moved his hand toward the pistol he wore in the cross-draw position.

Carson cocked his Colt and pointed it at a spot of

pink skin in the middle of the birthmark and near the center of the man's forehead.

The man froze.

"The rest of you get up there," Zeb said. "He can't shoot everybody."

Carson swung his pistol back toward Zeb. "Back away! First one touches a pistol. I shoot Zeb first and him next. Already got the trigger half pulled."

Zeb's face flushed deep red.

"Careful, boy." He motioned left and right. "Maybe y'all best back off a little."

Carson stepped one foot into the street, snatched the shotgun from beneath Bowean's right stirrup, and cocked both barrels. He waved the shotgun and the men around Zeb backed away. He holstered his Colt and switched the shotgun to his right hand. "This short little scattergun's loaded with double aught. I might not get you all, but I'll get enough."

His head on a swivel, he untied Zeb's horse and led him down the street.

Four of the men in the crowd, including the man with the birthmark, waited until Carson was out of shotgun range, then followed.

The sheriff's office was a small narrow brick building with one big multi-paned window. Carson pulled Zeb's horse close to the boardwalk, let the lead rope slide through his hand, uncocked the shotgun and rapped on the glass."

"Just come in," a gruff voice said.

"I'm Deputy Marshal Kettle. I need you to come outside."

Chair legs scraped and footsteps stomped across the floor. The sheriff flung the door open. When he saw Zeb, his red face turned white.

Carson pushed back the lapel of his coat enough to show his badge. "I need you to take this prisoner and identify the others."

The sheriff looked from Carson to Zeb.

"What you done now, Zebulon?"

Zeb smiled. "You know me, Cleve."

"Him and Jared Crusher and these men," Carson nodded toward the bodies on the packhorses, "and three others stole a herd of horses out of Texas."

Zeb shook his head.

"I understand there's paper on all of them. If you know them, you should know that."

The sheriff cleared his throat. "I'd like to help you, but the way things are around here, I don't think I'd keep Zeb in jail for more than a day or two before Jared skinned me."

Zeb smiled.

"Jared Crusher's on the run," Carson said. "and I'll be going after him."

The sheriff scraped a boot on the boardwalk. "He rode through here this morning, pushing a herd of horses. If he's going where I think he is, you'd best let him go."

Carson shook his head. "Can't do that. He's got a young girl with him."

Zeb spit. "It ain't a girl, Cleve. It's a picaninny."

Carson thought of little Tommy Green. His breath hung in his throat and his eyes narrowed. He took two strides and jammed the barrel of the shotgun into Zeb's belly, knocking the air from him and doubling him over.

The sheriff stepped forward. "No need for that!"

Carson cocked one barrel of the shotgun as he swung it toward the sheriff's face. "Stop right there. I haven't got time for this. You'll take this prisoner and then take these bodies to the undertaker and get them buried. You can bill Marshal Greer for the costs."

The sheriff shook his head. "I don't answer to Greer."

Deputy Marshal Gilmour Bowean's back at the post office and he'll be staying behind to make sure this prisoner doesn't go anywhere until I get back."

"Bowean's here?" the sheriff asked.

Zeb fought in enough breath to speak. "That big buck's all shot up. Let me go, and I'll take care of him right now."

Carson stepped back and, once again, jammed the shotgun into Zeb's midsection. "He's got a bad right arm, but that won't stop him from using this shotgun with his left."

The sheriff looked from Zeb to Carson. "Unshackle his legs and bring him in."

The sheriff's hand shook as he turned the key in the cell door.

"Don't do this, Cleve," Zeb said.

The sheriff hung his head and ushered Carson into the front office and closed the door to the hallway leading back to the two cells.

"I'll need you to get a message to Marshal Greer," Carson said.

*****

Carson hurried back to the post office and took the sorrel and the dun to the livery. "Rub down the dun and put him in a stall," he told the hostler, "I'll be back soon for the sorrel, but give him a pail of oats if you got them."

Minutes later, He lugged Bowean's saddle into the post office and through the door into the back.

Bowean uncocked his pistol with his left hand and laid it in his lap.

Wallace pulled tight a strip of clean bandage, tying a splint to Bowean's upper arm.

More sweat beaded on Bowean's already wet face.

Wallace looked up. "There's good news. I thought the bullet had shattered the arm, and we'd have to take it, but he must have broke it when he fell off his horse."

"Dove off," Bowean said with the hint of a pained smile.

Wallace continued. "If we can keep the infection at bay, he won't lose it. He says he's got to go after some girl, but he has to stay here, where I can keep it clean."

Bowean bowed his head and stared at his boots while Carson filled him in on the situation with the sheriff and then said, "I'd best get going."

Bowean nodded. "You go on then. I'm counting on you. So's that girl."

Suddenly despite his success with Lijah Penne, Carson felt uncertain. He'd had Nimrod and Ernie and the soldiers; now he was alone. "What should I do?"

"You know what to do. Trust yourself. Don't take any chances. That's what I did, took chances. I know better, but I got mad, and I got afraid for that girl, and I got careless." He glanced at his wounded arm. "You die out there and that girl's gonna suffer. If you have to, use your Sharps. Take Jared first, and the others will like as not turn tail."

Carson took a deep breath and tried to show confidence he didn't feel. "I'll bring her back."

"Fetch my scattergun and a pocketful of shells and I'll get over to the sheriff's office as soon as Mr. Wallace is done with me."

Wallace shook his head. "You need to rest."

Bowean looked at Carson. "There an empty cell over there?"

Carson nodded.

"I'll rest there."

Carson burned to get going, but he wanted to stay on the trail until he had the girl, no matter how long it took. He stopped at the mercantile and bought hardtack, bacon, beans, flour, lard, and baking powder. By the time he got back to the livery, the sorrel had finished his oats. He snugged the cinch, mounted, and headed out of town. He watched both sides of the road for signs the cow ponies had turned off.

A mile east, the tracks of the herd of unshod ponies split from the traffic on the road and turned north along a two-track trail. Though Jared and his men were likely miles away, Carson pulled the Yellowboy from its scabbard and followed.

Two miles north, it was clear the horses had passed under a high, pine-log gate. Two hundred yards in, a squat log cabin and long, log barn marked the ranch.

Carson rode to within a hundred yards and stopped. "Hello the house," he shouted. When there was no reply, he rode a little closer. "Hello the house!"

An old man carrying an Enfield and an old woman a shotgun, stepped out the door and onto the porch.

Knowing the range of the Enfield, Carson backed the sorrel a few strides, though not far enough to be safe.

"This here's private property," the old man shouted. "Git on down the road. We ain't accepting visitors today."

Carson slid back his jacket to show his badge. "I'm United States Deputy Marshal Kettle, and I'm following the wanted men and stolen horses that came through here."

The old man looked at the old woman, lowered his rifle, turned, and walked back into the house. The old woman followed without shutting the door.

Carson kept his Yellowboy in hand and his eyes on the door and the two windows on the front of the cabin, the only windows he could see. He stepped from the sorrel and ducked under one window and leaned against the log wall beside the door. "I just want to talk."

"Come in and talk, then," the old man said.

"You put those weapons away and make sure I can see your hands."

"The guns are leaning by the door."

Carson backed up enough to glance through the filthy window. The old couple sat at the table, coffee cups before them and an open, tobacco-juice-stained tin can between them. He leaned the Yellowboy against the wall, slid the thong from the hammer of his Colt, and loosened the pistol in its holster, then stepped into the one-room cabin.

The side of the old woman's wrinkly face was bruised and swollen.

"I'm looking for Jared Crusher and three other men. They drove a herd of horses through here today."

The old man nodded. "Four men rode through

here." He ducked his head and showed a nasty raw gash and goose egg peeking from between tufts of greasy hair on the top of his head, then he pointed to the bruise on the old woman's face. "Long enough to do this and rob us of our life's savings."

"Was there a girl with them?"

The old woman laid a claw-like hand on the old man's wrist and flicked her eyes toward him, then back at Carson. "Didn't see no girl."

"No thirteen-year-old negro girl?"

She shook her head. "No, sir, Mr. Deputy Sir. Herschel? You see a picaninny?"

The old man shook his head.

Carson was sure they were lying, but he didn't have time to argue. "Which way did they go?"

The old woman lifted the tin can to her lips and spit. "North into them hills."

Carson nodded and turned toward the door.

"You don't want to follow them back there," the old lady said.

"Why's that?"

The old woman met his eyes. "Folks back yonder ain't as friendly as we'uns. Especially to the law. Not too many lawdogs venture that way. Those that do, rarely come back."

The old man cleared his throat. "You'd best mount a posse, a big one, if you want to ride back there."

Bowean had told Carson about a deputy, years before, just after Bowean had joined the Marshals, who rode into this country looking for a man who'd murdered a whole family of freed, black folks, though they'd never found the bodies of the family's two young daughters. The deputy had never returned and neither his body, his horse, nor any other sign of him had ever been found. Carson backed to the door and glanced outside. "No time for that."

"You find them," the old lady said, "that gold their carrying belongs to us."

Carson swung onto the sorrel and, though he wanted to rush, headed north at a walk.

CHAPTER Seven

The sun beat down, drawing moisture from the recent rains out of the ground and the sweat from the skin of men and horses. Jared switched hands on the reins and moved the girl from his right arm to his left but found no relief from the ache of holding onto the limp body. He leaned forward, nuzzled past her hair, and clamped down on her ear until her sweet blood tickled his tongue.

For a moment, her back stiffened and relieved the pressure on his arm. He leaned back and licked his lips.

She thrashed and tried to throw herself from the horse.

"Stop! Or I'll bite it right off."

She threw herself one last time to the right, dragging his arm with her and forcing the gray pony to cut hard. It was all he could do to stay in the saddle.

He jerked the gray to a hard stop and threw her to the ground. Before she could scramble away, he was on her, raining blow after blow on her shoulders and the back of her head.

She twisted and clawed at the ground, dragging furrows in the wet sod, but the beating continued until she slumped and quit moving at all.

"That's enough," Burg said. "We got to ride."

Jared straightened his back and drove his left fist into the girl's side.

"Jared!" Burg said. "Let's go."

Jared rolled her face up.

"Leave her! Those deputies could be close and we're leaving a trail plain as day."

Jared looked up as if he'd heard Burg for the first time. "We'd best keep moving." He wrestled the girl over his shoulder and laid her over the gray's neck, just in front of the saddle. He climbed up behind her and wrapped his right hand in the back of her dress. "Let's ride."

A half hour later, Jared stopped the, now dripping, gray. He shook his right hand and winced at the burn of the blood returning to his fingers. He eased the cow pony out of the brush where he'd stopped and scanned the flats, ridges, and valleys they had recently crossed. Still no sign of pursuit. He glanced at the sky. Far to the west, huge thunderheads, black bottoms and shining white peaks, reached from the horizon to the blue sky. A good gully washer would wipe out their track, but he wouldn't count on that.

He led his men along the edge of a rocky ridge where the horses left almost no tracks. He stopped the little gray. "We'll split up here. Make sure you cover your tracks. Do some more stream riding and don't lead no deputies back to your homes."

"What about our share of the money?" Burg asked.

"Meet me at Ditch's cabin tomorrow. Not too early." He winked.

"What do we tell Bea?" Ankor asked.

Jared frowned and pressed his eyebrows together. "I haven't figured out what to tell her… about her pa. Stay away from her place. I'll tell her tomorrow."

*****

Jared fumbled with the latch and kicked open the door to Ditch's cabin. The remnants of spoiled food and unwashed bodies flooded out with a wave of stifling hot air.

He glanced down at the girl in his arms, and he carried her through the door. "Just like a new bride," he said with a little laugh.

The girl's eyes fluttered, then opened toward the ceiling.

Jared smiled. "There she is."

Her body jerked once and then again. She retched and spewed putrid yellow bile mixed with lines of bright, red blood, onto the hard, dirt floor.

He danced back but not before the slimy vomit splashed onto his boots and pants. He gagged. "Why'd you do that? I guess you'll clean that up."

She looked at him with unfocused eyes.

He backed away from the bile on the floor and leaned over to set her on her feet.

Another stream of yellow spewed from her body and coated his arm.

He retched at the smell and dropped her feet. "You clean that up."

She sagged and fell into the mess on the floor. Gone again.

*****

Hours later, he poured another glug of corn, from the jug Ditch always kept, into a tin cup. This wasn't at all how he'd seen things unfolding. After making such a mess, the girl hadn't opened her eyes, and her breath came in fits and starts. He lifted the lantern from the middle of the table. She hadn't moved. She wasn't dead yet, but there was blood mixed with her foul vomit. Maybe he'd killed her. He set down the lantern, slugged back the whiskey, and dropped his face into his hands.

The door burst open. He lifted his head from the table. The bright morning sunshine blinded him.

"Jared?" Bea said in a bright voice as she entered the cabin. "Why didn't you...?"

She plugged her nose and glanced down. "Are you all right? You sick?"

Not Bea. How had she found him?

She stepped out of the remnants of Hannah's vomit, most of the liquid either soaked into the dirt floor, or dried into the air, and slapped the tin cup across the room. "I see what the problem is. Where's Ditch? Where's my Pa?"

What could he say? He had to think, but his thoughts oozed like cool molasses. "I... I just didn't know how to tell you."

Her voice trembled. "Jared? Tell me what? Where's my pa?"

"That's why I didn't come last night..."

Hannah moaned.

Bea stepped out of the light beaming in the door and clenched her fists. "I see why you didn't come." She marched over to the cot where Hannah lay blinking her eyes. "Who are you?"

Hannah looked up wide-eyed and cowered back against the wall.

Jared tipped back the jug and drained the last two swallows. He wiped his mouth with his sleeve, rubbing dried bile across his lips. His stomach flipped but he held the whiskey down. "She ain't a wench. She's a picaninny we found along the trail. Somebody give her a beating and left her to die. I didn't know if she'd make it to my ma's so I brung her here."

Bea leaned close to Hannah. "Light that lamp."

Jared turned up the wick and lit the lamp.

Bea snatched it from his hands. "Oh my, she is just a girl, and she's been sorely abused." She cast hard eyes on Jared, then turned back to the girl. "What's your name, child?"

Hannah pressed herself harder against the wall, then glanced toward the door and Jared. Tears welled in her eyes. "Please, help me. Please."

Bea reached out a hand to stroke Hanna's head, but the girl reeled back into the corner.

"I won't hurt you. Who did this?"

Hannah looked past Bea.

Jared glared a silent warning. He had to stop the girl from telling what he'd done. "I'm so sorry, Bea. Your pa and Ditch are dead."

Bea spun around. At first, he thought she might strike him, but her body slumped, and her face melted into tears. She threw her arms around his neck, pressed his head to her shoulder, and sobbed.

He hugged her with one arm, narrowed his eyes

and shook his head over Bea's shoulder toward Hannah.

"Hold me like you mean it," Bea said.

"My other arm's a mess."

"I don't care," Bea said. "Tell me what happened."

He held her a minute and gathered his thoughts. "Ditch had another jug stashed away. I think we could both use a snort."

She nodded and moved to the table and sat.

Jared picked up his cup from the floor and rinsed a second cup for Bea with a slosh of whiskey that he tossed out the open door.

After pouring them each a half cupful, he began, "We got a nice bunch of Texas cow ponies, the one's Burg saw. Got away without a hitch. There was a big storm brewing, blowing in fast, but we got down into the Red before we even saw anybody. We was just across, when the river rose like it was alive. I suppose from the storms to the west."

"I reckon we'd be swinging by now, or drowned, had we not made it across when we did. That rancher and his men pulled up on the south shore, and we knew watching the sweeper trees and such rolling along in that high water, they'd never get across for days, so we just waved and holed up 'til morning and the worst of the storm was over."

"What happened to my pa?"

"I'm getting there. Next morning, we high-tailed it out of there. That's when it happened. That's when that filthy buck, Gilmour Bowean, and passel of other deputies ambushed us."

He emptied his cup while he gathered his thoughts. There was no harm in painting Zeke a hero. "The first volley cut down Ditch and Bragger Bill.

They got your pa's horse too, but your pa come away unharmed. He waved us on and turned on them dirty sneaks, firing his Winchester."

"Bullets was flying everywhere, but your pa held them deputies off us, 'til we got them ponies away. I sent the rest on and turned back to fetch your pa. Last I saw, Bowean stepped out and gut shot him, then he walked up smiling and shot him in the head."

"I was about to ride down and kill that nigra, when Uncle Zeb rode in front of my horse and stopped me. Much as I wanted to go, he was right."

"Where is Uncle Zeb? I didn't see his horse when I rode by his cabin."

Jared shook his head. He would have to be sure all the boys told the same story. "Caint say if he's dead or alive. We went back that night to catch Bowean. Thought we could tar and feather him, then string him up for all to see. But he was waiting. I think the deputies might have caught Uncle Zeb. I'll send Cousin Frankie to town to talk to Cleve and find out. If they've got him, we'll get him back."

Bea raised her face from her hands. "I want you to kill that Deputy Bowean."

Jared pressed his lips together in a half smile. "Already done. Shot him myself."

Bea grabbed his forearm and met his eyes. "Thank you." She glanced out the door. "We need to tell your ma. I expect she'll want to hear it from you."

"Let's go then," he said.

"What about her?" Bea asked.

He took a deep breath and gathered his thoughts. "Don't think she could stand the ride. She's addled and might run off and get lost. We'll lock her in here, shutter up the windows, and once we've seen your ma, I'll come back and tend to her. I've got half a notion I know where her people live. I'll get her back to her folks. Let them tend to her."

"Nonsense," Bea said. "Memaw's tinctures will do her a world more good than any darky potions. Besides, I expect Memaw will need something to do. The girl can ride with me. She's a bit of a thing. I'll hold her."

Jared's face fell. Somehow, he had to stop the girl from talking. He should have cut out her tongue. "She loses her head again; she'll be too much for you. She can ride with me."

CHAPTER Eight

Carson rode past the cabin and beyond the barn. He glanced west at the clouds building on the horizon. He needed to find the men before the rains wiped out their tracks.

A grassy pasture stretched across the shallow valley. A few skinny, spotted cows and calves lay in the deep grass close to the barn, chewing their cuds and enjoying the warm sun. On the far side of the clearing, a herd of grazing horses spread across the grass.

A well-beaten two-track path, almost a road, crossed the pasture and wound toward the treeline. He recognized one of the horses, a black and white pinto, with a black spot on his hip that looked like a bear. These were the Texas cow ponies. Four horses, still bearing the salt-sweat lines from being unsaddled and unbrushed, stood together away from the others. He galloped closer, stopping out of Winchester range of the pine and oak trees marking the end of the meadow. He wouldn't make Bowean's mistake.

With his field glasses, he scanned the trees, rode closer and scanned again. Seeing no sign of men or horses in the trees, he pushed the sorrel into a lope, ducking low and cutting left and right.

He stopped at the treeline and breathed a sigh. The men had moved on. The path led into the trees and the tracks of four unshod horses followed the well-beaten track up the gentle slope. He would have to do something about the stolen cow ponies, but not until he had the girl back.

He followed the deep hoof prints at a trot, stopping often to check potential ambush sites. At each stop, he glanced west at the storm clouds rolling toward him. He burned to rush forward, but he pressed down the desire and maintained his caution.

He followed the tracks to a brushy ridge and found a little flat bench of land where the men and horses had stopped. From there, the tracks led to a rocky ridge. He had to slow to a walk and eventually dismount to find where the horses had dislodged a rock here and there.

A chilly breeze rose and cooled his cheeks. To the west, streaks of rain reached like long fingers from the clouds to the ground. A cloud lit up. Carson counted. One and, two and, three and, four and, five and, six and, seven. Thunder sounded. Seven miles.

He hurried to the end of the rocky section. One set of hoof prints, the only ones he could find, descended the hill, and disappeared into a low clump of sweetshrub. He scoured the surrounding earth with his eyes. What if they'd split up? How would he find the girl?

Another flash of light followed by thunder. He had to make a choice. A bird in hand, his father always said. He brushed around the sweetshrub, smelling the faint hint of strawberry that gave the shrub its name, found the hoofprints, and followed them along a low pine-covered ridge and finally into a small rocky stream. He knew the trick. Ride into the stream to cover your tracks, but with the rain coming, he needed to hurry and find where the horse had left the stream. He dismounted and stepped to the edge of the babbling water, but nothing showed on the rocky bottom.

Another thunderclap, this one closer.

He mounted, crossed the stream, and looked left and right, before turning the sorrel downstream.

Two hundred yards along, he found where the horse had left the stream and continued along the sidehill. He took a deep breath and pushed the sorrel into a fast trot.

Focused as he was on the tracks, the first icy drops of rain shocked him. Within less than a minute, the sky opened and, even among the pine, oak, and hickory, he and the sorrel were drenched. He mentally marked a large broken-topped pine, as far along the direction of the tracks as he could see, then he pulled the sorrel in under the branches and leaves of the closest big oak.

He dismounted and pressed himself against the rough bark on the downwind side of the tree. The sorrel pushed his head in against him and he scratched the white crescent on the horse's forehead. "If this keeps up, there'll be no tracks to follow. What do we do then?" he asked, but the sorrel's only answer was to push his head closer for more scratching.

Carson knew deputies like Bowean sometimes paid

money, or traded food for information, but truth be told, he had no idea where he was or where he might find people. And if he found them, he had no way of knowing if they were friendly to Jared Crusher or, if, as the old couple had said, they were unfriendly to lawmen.

The storm raged for an hour. When it slowed and subsided, the west wind ripped at his coat and the sorrel's mane and tail. The late afternoon sun sparkled in rainbow hues from the droplets being blown from the trees. He brushed the beaded water from the seat of his well-oiled saddle, mounted, and headed toward the broken tree, hoping the men had also been forced to wait out the storm and would continue in the same direction.

With the day quickly fading, he pushed the sorrel into a fast trot. He stopped beside the broken pine. Four or five miles to the north, a long ridge stretched as far as he could see from east to west. After checking the valley between for any signs of life, he headed for the ridge. Maybe he could see something from there.

The sun had disappeared on the western horizon, but still pushed a crescent of light into the now-clear sky. Carson dismounted and eased himself to the crest of the ridge. His field glasses gathered more light than his eyes, but another ridge, about a mile north, blocked his view and he found nothing in the shallow valley between.

A flicker of motion caught his eye. A whitetail spike stepped from behind a thick clump of brush.

Carson froze.

The buck glanced left and right, then flicked his tail and dropped his nose into the grass.

We're he not on a manhunt, Carson might have shot the young animal. As it was, he backed down the hill, found a semi-dry spot to stretch out his bedroll, and ate a cold supper of hardtack and cold beans.

He tossed and turned until he feared he wouldn't sleep at all. He dug twigs and tiny stones from beneath his bedroll and scratched a hole for his hips, but sleep wouldn't come.

What did Jared Crusher want with the girl?

Surely, he knew she would draw the deputies on, even more than the horses. Or did he?

Even after the war, many people still thought of people with black skin as livestock. Was that it? Did he want to enslave her?

It really didn't matter why he'd taken her, Carson had to find a way to free the girl and return her to her brother and capture all four remaining outlaws. Not only had they killed her parents and taken her and the horses, but they'd also shot Bowean.

Though his body ached for rest, his mind kept spinning until something rustled in the leaf litter and jerked him from his fretful dreams. Heart pounding, he half opened his eyes and slid his hand until his fingers found the smooth wooden grip of his Colt. He took the pistol in his hand and turned, first his eyes, and then his head toward the sound.

He smiled. A momma skunk and six babies rooted through the oak leaves looking for bugs. The sorrel snorted and the momma skunk stomped and hissed, and her tail snapped up in a flash of white.

Carson froze.

The sorrel stomped a foot.

The momma skunk arched her back.

"Easy, boy," Carson whispered. "It's all right."

The sorrel snorted louder and bounced on his front feet toward the skunk.

She arched even higher, and Carson ducked his head under his oilskin tarp.

Even under the tarp, he squeezed shut his eyes, nose, and mouth to avoid the pungent smell. When he could no longer stand the closed air under the tarp, he threw it back and opened his eyes. Through a river of tears, he searched for the skunks, but they were gone. He tried for a shallow breath, then hacked and coughed until he retched and spewed the remains of his meager supper on the ground.

The sorrel leaned back on his haunches and rubbed his face first on one foreleg, then the other.

Carson crawled from his bed, leaned against the oak, and found some fresher air. The sorrel snorted and stomped. A belly laugh rumbled up from Carson's core. He tried to hold it in, but it burst out, and all he could do was try to hold the sound down.

By the time he'd gained control, the sorrel stood still, his head hanging and his ears drooping. Carson scooped up handfuls of leaves and moss and did his best to scrub the stink from the foot of his tarp and from the sorrel's entire front.

"I guess we truly are stinkin' deputies now," he said with a chuckle.

The eastern sky lightened, and there was no chance of further sleep. Carson longed for a cup or two of coffee, but he remembered Bowean's caution about smoke when they'd camped near the Red River, and not knowing the terrain or who might be about, decided not to risk a fire.

At first, he could barely stand to eat with the reek on the air, but after a few minutes, his nose grew accustomed to the smell, and he took the edge off of his hunger with a slab of jerky and more hardtack.

As soon as the woods before him brightened enough for him to see any tracks, he saddled the sorrel and headed north toward the next ridge.

At first it looked like a haze over the ridge in the still morning air. As he climbed higher, it was columns of smoke rising from more than a dozen fires, until they spread and joined into the low, thin cloud he'd first seen.

He left the sorrel and climbed to the crest. There were no houses visible, but the columns of smoke rose above the treetops from fires, well spread out across two to three miles from east to west. It had to be a community of farmhouses, each with someone cooking their breakfast. His mouth watered at the thought of the bacon, flour, and lard in his saddlebags.

He needed a better view. He pulled out another chunk of jerky, mounted, and circled the ridge to the east and downwind of what must be the farm community.

He wound down through the pines and into a dense oak and hickory forest. A rooster crowed, and he slowed. The crack of an axe stopped him. He waited. Crack! Crack! Crack!

He pressed forward, staying to any low ground he could find. Through the trees, he spotted a small clapboard cabin in a little clearing. The warped siding on the cabin had seen a coat of whitewash, but not recently. An equally run-down hen house and a pigpen stood between the cabin and a rocky field of spindly corn.

Easing the sorrel in behind a thick-branched,

young hickory, he waited and watched. There was an old mule in a pasture behind a log barn, a barn too small to hold more than two horses. There were no horses in sight, but before he rode in, he needed to be sure Jared Crusher or any of his men weren't around.

A young woman in a faded blue dress and matching bonnet stepped out the door of the cabin carrying a wooden pail and entered the barn. After twenty minutes, a boney, tan-colored milk cow left the back of the barn and joined the mule in the pasture.

The woman carried her pail of milk from the barn and toward the house. She left the barn door open. There were no horses inside. As she entered the cabin, a man, also young and thin, wearing a canvas shirt and trousers and bare feet stepped out carrying a different pail.

Hogs squealed and grunted as he rounded the house and poured milk into their trough.

Just as the man was about to enter the house, Carson took a deep breath. "Hello the house," he shouted.

The man ducked through the door, then peeked his head out. "Who's out there?"

"Name's Carson. I'm looking for a friend."

The man's head disappeared, then reappeared. "We don't know no Carson. Who you be looking for?"

"Can I ride up?" Carson asked. "I mean you no harm."

"Come on up, then. No funny stuff. I got my scattergun here."

Carson shoved the thong from the trigger of his Colt, then eased the sorrel out from behind the hickory tree.

Once Carson was halfway to the house and well

clear of the trees, the man stepped half out of the door. "You all alone?"

Carson nodded. "Yes, sir."

The man grinned and turned back to the house. "Hear that honey, He called me sir."

When Carson was twenty yards from the house, the man stepped onto the porch and pointed the shotgun.

Without moving his head, Carson scanned left and right for something that would shield him from a shotgun blast. He should have thought of that before riding in. He wanted to pull his Colt and even the odds, but it was too late for that. "Would you mind pointing that away from my face? I mean you no harm and I'd hate for you to slip."

The man glanced back into the house. "Hear that, honey? He don't enjoy looking down Birdie's gullet."

Carson thought of spurring the sorrel to one side and pulling his Colt, but at twenty yards, the shotgun was likely to take him, even if he was quick to pull the Colt, and quick draws were not his strong point. Besides, he needed answers.

He smiled. "Could I ride in and water my horse, maybe fill my canteen?"

The man lowered the shotgun and nodded as Carson rode by toward the water trough, half in and half out of the pasture holding the mule and cow. The man waved his hand in front of his face. "Uuugh! You been skunk sprayed."

Carson smiled and nodded. "Horse spooked a momma skunk back yonder."

The woman called from the house, "See if he's et."

A few minutes later, Carson sat at the far end of

the porch savoring a bowl of corn grits, slathered with rich, heavy cream and dark, pine honey.

The man shoveled the contents of his bowl into his mouth, wiped his mouth on his dirty sleeve, and said, "Name's Nate. You?"

Carson paused, he doubted anyone down here would have heard of him, but to be safe, he said, "Nimrod. Nimrod Carson."

The woman smiled. "Good bible name. Now what brings you to our hills, Mr. Nimrod Carson?"

Carson's mind raced. He thought of what the old couple had said about these people and lawmen. What should he..., what could he tell them?

CHAPTER Nine

They wound through pines, then down into the hickory and oak. The wide trail narrowed. Bea rode ahead and led the way down the steep hill. Jared slowed the gray horse until there was at least thirty yards between him and Bea.

Jared's mind raced. He couldn't let Bea know the dark things filling his thoughts and dreams. That knowledge had to wait until after they were married and maybe had a baby on the way.

He pulled Hannah close and whispered in her ear. "You say you don't know who beat you. You understand?"

She stared straight ahead.

He grabbed a fold of her skin and twisted.

She winced and nodded.

"Say your folks live toward Rocky Comfort." He grabbed the same fold of skin, but before he could twist, she whispered, "Yes, suh."

Before long, hound dogs bayed, and they broke into a large clearing. The white clapboard house had a long front porch with six low-slung wooden chairs lined up along the front wall.

A gray-haired woman sat in a chair close to the door. Her face broke into a broad, toothy grin. "It's okay, Abe, it's just Miss Beatrice and my baby."

A young man of around twelve or thirteen burst from the house. He touched his brow and nodded as he ran by Bea. "Miss Beatrice." Then he skidded to a stop beside Jared. "Who's that?"

Jared forced a brief smile, then wiped it away. "That's a picaninny we found beat along the trail. Like a bird with a broken wing, we brought her to Memaw to see if she can fix her up. But first we got bad news."

Memaw pushed out of her chair and looked from Bea to Jared and back. "Who'd we lose?"

Bea leaped from her horse, ran to the old woman, and threw her arms around her. "My pa's gone, and Ditch and Bragger Bill, and maybe Uncle Zeb."

Jared slid Hannah to the ground and held the back of her arm, while the women rocked and cried.

After a moment, Memaw pushed back. "I told those two old fools they was too old to go off gallivanting. But they loved it so." She pulled a clean handkerchief from a pocket in her crisp, clean dress, wiped her eyes, and blew her nose. "Who killed them?"

Jared lowered his eyes. "That blackheart Gilmour Bowean."

Memaw clutched at the heavy pendant hanging under her shirt from the gold chain around her neck. Her sad eyes narrowed. "He coming after you?"

Jared looked up. "No, ma'am. I shot him myself."

"Bowean kill Zeb too?"

"No, ma'am. We went back to catch Bowean. We was gonna string him up for killing Ditch and Bragger Bill..."

Memaw stood tall, her eyes narrow and fierce.

Bile rose in Jared's throat. He swallowed it back. "Me and Zeke and Zeb went back, and that was when Bowean shot Zeke and caught Zeb. Was later I killed him."

"I thought I'd send Cousin Frankie to town and find out from Cleve if they've got him locked up somewhere." He kicked the dirt.

Memaw turned to the young boy. "Abe, run fetch Frankie."

"Awe, Memaw. I wanna stay and watch you patch up that picaninny."

"Come here," Memaw said. Abe shuffled to her side. She pulled him close. "You hurry back with Frankie. Tell him to bring his horse, and then I'll need you to sound the alarm. Jared will saddle Blackie for you. Once you're done, I'll show you exactly what I did for this poor child. Go on now."

Abe grinned, turned, and sprinted across the yard toward a trail leading through the trees.

She turned back to Jared. "Did you get the horses?"

He nodded. "Thirty-three head. This is one of them."

"Get paid for 'em?" Memaw asked.

"Yes, ma'am. Agnes and Herschel weren't keen on taking them, but I got the gold right here in my saddlebag." He turned and, keeping one hand on Hannah, dug out the pouch of coins.

She held out her hand. "You pay off the other boys?"

"Not yet."

She smiled, then glanced at his knuckles and looked him in the eyes. "Found her along the road already beat, did you?"

He dropped his eyes to the ground. "Yes, ma'am. Something like that."

Memaw pushed Jared's hand from Hannah's arm. "Come with me, child." She turned toward the house.

Jared followed, he wanted to keep Hannah in earshot.

Memaw turned. "Won't need you for this. Put those horses up and saddle Blackie for Abe."

"I'd like to watch you patch up that child."

"How many deputies you figure gonna come? By all accounts, that Bowean was some kind a hero? We need to prepare. You'd best be getting ready to ride. You can help Abe warn folks, then you and the boys gonna need to hole up for a good while."

Jared tied the gray and Bea's dun in the big white barn and gave them each a scoop of corn. He climbed the ladder to the loft and forked hay through the holes in the loft floor and into the horses' mangers. He would stick to his story, that he knew where Hannah's folks were, and he would take her with him to O'Neal's old cabin and wait until the deputies had shot their wads and moved on.

He sneaked into the back door and peeked into the room, where Memaw and Bea bathed Hannah's scrapes and bruises.

Without looking up, Memaw said, "You go on and saddle a pack horse and load up enough food and such for you and the boys to stay out for a month. Send Frankie to town. Tell him to find out if Zeb's in jail and send Abe east to warn folks and you spread the word west while you gather your boys, then you four hightail it to O'Neal's old cabin. Don't come back until I send for you. If I need you to go for Zeb, I'll send Abe."

He stood there staring at Hannah.

"Go on. You got your orders. Now, git!" she said.

Bea jumped up, ran to him, and threw her arms around him. "Wish I could come with you," she said, then she leaned in and nibbled on his ear. She lowered her voice until he could barely hear her. "I'll come if I can."

He took her hand and led her out the back door. "Nice as that sounds, be too dangerous. Soon as the deputies leave, we'll be together." He lifted his chin and kissed her mouth.

"Miss you already," she said.

"Could you finish packing the packhorse?" he said, "while I fetch the boys."

She nodded, then squeezed him close.

He could barely breathe and pulled away. "I best get moving... 'Fore them deputies get here."

An hour later, he led Burg, Ankor, and Willy into Memaw's yard. "Ankor, you take the packhorse," he said as he leaped to the ground and ran through the front door.

"Hush," Memaw said. "She's sleeping."

"I know where her folks live. I thought I'd drop her there, while we was out riding."

Memaw furrowed her brow and shook her head. "I believe you've done enough for that child."

His heart sank. "Don't believe no lies no picaninny tells."

Memaw took his hand and ran his thumb over his knuckles. "Just like your pa, God rest him." She dropped his hand. "She hasn't uttered a word. But you leave her here." She hugged him and kissed his cheek. "Go on now. Git. I'll send for you if I need you, or when it's safe."

His shoulders slumped as excitement drained from his body like wheat from a mouse-chewed sack. He shuffled out the front door.

Abe galloped into the yard on his black pony. "There's a stranger at Turlock's."

Jared looked over Abe's shoulder. "What's he look like?"

Abe shrugged.

"Young? Old?"

"Older than me, but not as old as you."

"What color's his hair?"

Abe shrugged again. "He had a hat on, but I reckon maybe like Bea's only a little darker."

"Did you see his horse?"

Abe nodded.

"And?"

"Kinda red, like Peach."

"Sorrel?"

Abe nodded. "He's got a rifle on each side of his saddle. And he stinks."

"Stinks?"

"Said he got skunk sprayed."

Eyes wide and cheeks flushed, Bea stepped out the front door and ran to Jared.

Memaw followed close behind. "Sounds like a deputy. You boys ride. Take the trail past McNally's then circle north. Tell McNally to keep an eye out."

That night, while the other boys drank and played cards, Jared smoked and paced the floor of the one-room cabin. As he finished one cigarette, he rolled another and lit it from the one he already smoked, then he tossed the butt onto the floor and ground it under his boot.

Ankor glanced up. "You'll be out of tobacco by tomorrow, you keep that up."

Jared glared. "And you'll be outta whiskey." He stomped to the door.

"Where you going?" Burg asked.

"I need some fresh air."

Three hours later, the cabin door opened. Willy stood in the doorway. "You gonna stay out there all night?"

"Might!" Jared said.

Without another word, Willy closed the door, and the cabin went dark.

Jared waited another thirty minutes. He wandered toward the horses. It was less than two hours back to the house. He could be there and back, and have the girl stashed in the old cabin in the next hollow, before these drunks woke up.

He placed one foot on the bottom rung of the corral, then turned, stomped into the cabin, and flopped onto his bunk.

The next morning, he rose while the rest slept, took his rifle, and climbed the low hill behind the cabin and over into the hollow on the other side.

He pushed through dense brush, grown up over the years the place had been abandoned. The old log cabin hadn't changed much since he'd found it while tracking a wounded buck, or in the year since he'd last been here with Bea. The wooden door scraped across the plank floor as he shoved his way in. Even after what must have been decades, the cypress shingles kept things inside dry. A fine coat of dust covered everything, including the bed where he'd first told Bea he loved her, and she'd first given herself to him.

That day, he thought she'd always be enough, but it wasn't long before he realized she wouldn't. He hoped she'd be like Memaw had been with his Papaw. Give him strong sons and let him take his special pleasures whenever the need grew too strong.

He smiled. He'd never felt the need like he felt it today.

He pulled the blankets from the bed, carried them to the porch, shook out the dust, and tossed them back onto the mattress. Next, he checked the cans of beans and beef on the shelves. All seemed sound. He shook the lantern on the little table. Still half full of kerosene. He chopped a few armfuls of wood, then dropped onto the bed and slept away the afternoon.

On his way back to the boys, he heard the keekee, keekees of a flock of wild turkeys. He stepped from his horse and pulled his rifle, then shoved it back and tied the gray.

As he reached the peak of the rise, he loosened his Colts in their holsters, hovered his hand over the butts, and crept over the hill.

The turkeys erupted in a cacophony of cries and beating wings. In one smooth motion, he drew his right pistol and fired. A big hen dropped from the sky and lay fluttering on the ground.

Back at O'Neal's old cabin, the boys stepped outside at the sound of his horse.

Burg said, "Where the hell you been? We was afraid the deputies got you."

Still proud of the shot he'd made, Jared turned the gray until the boys could see the turkey, then tossed it at Burg's feet. "Some of us caint sleep all day. I thought we could use some fresh meat. Ankor, I ketched it, you clean it."

Ankor picked up the carcass. "Stinks. You gut shot it."

Blood rushed to Jared's face. "Shot it on the fly... with my six shooter. Rinse it in the creek."

The cabin filled with mouth-watering smells as Willy fried strips of turkey breast with potatoes and an onion Bea had packed for them. Jared looked in, then returned to his spot outside the door and rolled another cigarette.

When the food was ready, he sat with the boys, but barely touched his food.

Burg tapped the side of Jared's plate with his fork. "You gonna eat that?"

Jared shook his head and pushed the plate away. Burg caught the rim with his fork and slid the plate beside his own.

Not long after supper the boys, one by one, drifted to their beds, no doubt still feeling the effects of the night before.

Jared waited until the snoring and heavy breathing settled into a steady rhythm, then left the cabin and saddled the gray.

CHAPTER Ten

Carson leaned back against the chair and enjoyed the grits. His mother always served her grits with butter and salt. This bowlful tasted more like a sweet dessert. Carson savored a spoonful on his tongue and liked it just fine.

Nate held his bowl to his lips and scooped the grits into his mouth with his spoon.

Wanting to think, and to savor the sweetness, Carson picked up his coffee and sipped. Another taste of honey and cream, so different from the strong bitter black brew that Bowean boiled out on the trail.

The wind swirled and pungent skunk perfume wafted under the porch roof. Carson, smelling of skunk himself, barely noticed the change, but Nate and his missus both fanned their noses. Carson tipped his bowl, shoveled in the last of his grits, and set the bowl on the stump beside his rustic wooden chair.

As much as he wanted to come out and ask about Jared, he needed a better plan. "Let me move my horse, then maybe y'all can help me find my friend."

Nate smiled. "Good idea."

Carson moved the horse around to the back of the cabin and tied him to the fence near the mule and the cow.

When Carson returned, Nate tipped a tan and brown jug and poured a glug of whiskey into Carson's coffee. "Tastes fine with coffee and cream and honey."

Carson smiled and sipped. The strong whiskey burned going down and the fumes rising in the back of his throat brought a tear to his eye. He raised the cup. "Does." He hesitated, wondering what to say to these strangers. Odds were, they knew Jared Crusher and they could even be friends or family. "My friend's name's Jared. He said he hails from these parts."

Nate looked from his wife to his shotgun, leaned against the wall, then back at Carson. "What kind of rifle you got there? The one with the glass?"

"Sharps," Carson said.

"Not too many carry two rifles in these parts."

"I'm on my way west to try my hand at buffalo hunting. They say a man can earn a stake if he can shoot."

Nate again glanced at his wife. "And how'd you come to be friends with this Jared fella?"

Carson looked up at the sky, then back at the couple. "Well, truth be told, we met in the saloon in Rocky Comfort."

"And you rode all the way out here to see a fella you just met? You make friends right quick, Mr. Carson."

Carson smiled. "I suppose he must be a friend. I loaned him money. After we'd shared some whiskey and some laughter, he wandered off into a game of cards. After a time, he called me over and showed me his hand, three aces. Then he asked for a small loan so he could raise.

I gave him twenty dollars, sure the man across the table would fold at such a bet.

The man looked at his stack of bills and gold coins, turned to the girl standing at his shoulder, and said, 'Merly, how much do I have there?'

When the girl finished counting, the man shoved in $260.00.

I took a deep breath and started for the bar, but Jared called me back. 'Stake me and I'll give you half the winnings. You saw my cards. I can't lose.'

I shook my head. 'It's too much. I'm no gambler.'

Jared smiled and said, 'These boys all know me. They'll tell you I'm good for it. We're just on our way to pick up a herd of good Texas cow ponies, already bought and paid for. Even if I lose, it'll only be a few days before I can pay you with interest.'

I looked around and the men all smiled and nodded.

Even with everything I'd save for my trip, I was short, but I pulled out my granddaddy's gold watch and plopped it down on the pile.

The fancy man nodded and dropped three twos on the table. Jared threw down his three aces, a king, and a jack, and reached for the pile.

The fancy man threw down two threes.

Carson pulled the gold watch he had taken from Zeke from his pocket, then quickly tucked it away. The fancy man handed me back my grandaddy's watch as he left."

Carson ran his eyes from Nate to his wife, trying to gauge their reaction. "I guess I missed Jared when they rode through Rocky Comfort with the horses, so now I'm here to get my money." He smiled his biggest smile. "Jared's probably just settling the ponies before he comes back, but I'm keen to head west."

He glanced from Nate to his woman, hoping they believed his tale, the tallest he'd ever told.

Hoof beats drew their eyes and a red-headed boy on a black pony loped into the yard. "Uncle Nate. Aunt Elsie. Memaw sent me to..." He glanced at Carson and his eyes opened wide. Nate shook his head.

"Come on inside, Abe. It'd be rude to talk family business in front of our new friend Nimrod here."

The boy ducked his head and watched his bare feet as he shuffled toward the cabin. His head came up. "The dogs get skunked?"

His aunt laughed and looked at Carson. "No, that'd be Mr. Carson."

The boy glanced at Carson as he left the cabin.

Carson smiled, but the boy had already looked away.

The boy swung onto the pony and tore off the way he'd come, reins whipping left and right and his bare heels flapping like wings.

Nate came out of the cabin grinning and slapped Carson on the shoulder. "Yours is a mighty sad tale. Sorry we caint help, but we'uns know everyone around these parts and there's no Jared."

Carson was about to argue, but caught himself and said, "I'm sorry to hear that. I must have been misinformed. I'd best be on my way." He tipped his hat. "Thank you for the breakfast, ma'am. It was delicious."

He rode back the way he'd come. He'd been sure

Nate and Elsie believed his story and knew Jared, but something the boy said had changed their minds. Once well clear of Nate's cabin, he dismounted and let his horse graze. He needed to think.

The boy had looked shocked to see him, and Nate had come out of the cabin friendlier. Much friendlier. The boy had ridden in from the northwest with his message and left the same way in a big hurry.

His best bet was to ride back far enough to hide his tracks on the rocky ridge. Then once it was dark, he could use every skill his father taught him stalking whitetails, to sneak up on the cabins in the valley and find Jared and the girl.

When he came to the small creek, he turned downstream, rode around the first bend, then rode out of the water and up the north bank. He stopped and backed the sorrel back into the water and headed upstream. He scrambled the sorrel up a five-foot steep, but sloped-back, waterfall. After a few more strides upstream, he left the water and headed south toward the rocky ridge.

He rode along the rocks and, with a quick prayer that he find no snakes, ducked his face and pushed the sorrel into a thick clump of low-growing evergreens. Cedar dust tickled his nose, and he choked back a sneeze. On the far side of the ridge, he paused and listened, then rode down a draw and up the other side into a spread-out stand of hickory on top of a small hill.

He picketed the sorrel at the bottom of the hill, in a grassy spot surrounded on three sides by low-growing shrubs and larger trees. He found a sunny spot beside a large rock and settled in to wait for dark. Soon, with the warmth of the sun and the strain of the past few days, his eyes blinked longer and longer, until he fell asleep.

A chilly breeze tugged at his hair and drew him from his dreams. He listened before he opened his eyes. The trees cast long shadows and clouds on the western horizon glowed in pinks and oranges. His stomach grumbled.

He checked all around, then climbed the hill with his field glasses and glassed any open area in sight. Seeing nothing, he decided to risk a fire.

He heated a can of beans and made a pot of coffee. It was going to be a long night. The beans were sweet and rich, but the coffee seemed harsh compared to the honey and cream-laced concoction he had consumed that morning.

His supper finished, he wiped the pan with a tuft of dry grass, dumped the coffee grounds from his coffee pot, and packed everything away. He saddled the sorrel, then leaving him tied, climbed the hill for one last look around.

He saw two groups of whitetail deer, come out to feed in the twilight, but no other creatures, two-legged or four. He pushed up to his feet, trotted down the hill, and mounted. Instead of going back the way he'd come, he cut northwest. That was the way the boy on the pony had ridden.

He stopped at the creek, filled his canteen, and let the sorrel drink.

Woooo! Wooo! Woo!

Baying hounds. Someone was out hunting. He remembered the bear hunts on dark nights with his father, and especially the black night when he had wounded a treed bear. The bear tumbled to the ground and nearly gutted their old hound on its way past them and into the heavy underbrush.

He mounted and rode through the water, then paused again and listened. The baying sounded closer. Whatever they were tracking was coming his way, but unless they changed direction, they would pass to the east, somewhere along the trail he had followed to Nate's cabin.

Was it possible? Were they hunting him? He spun the sorrel around, rode back into the creek, and splashed through the water until he could no longer see potential hazards.

He had a decision to make. Either ride away, far and fast, leaving the dogs in his dust and give the impression he had left the area and returned to Rocky Comfort, or try to evade the dogs and stay on the hunt for Jared and the girl.

As much as he wanted to stay after Jared and the girl, he thought it better that they think he left the area. He crossed back over the creek and picked his way through the shadows to the rocky ridge. The baying now came from near the creek below and lantern light bounced off the trees.

The moon rose and cast pale light on the trail. He pushed the sorrel into a trot and made his way back toward the ranch and town.

CHAPTER Eleven

Jared loved the night. Always had. But tonight, he had other things on his mind. His body buzzed with excitement, but he needed to be patient and careful, with at least one deputy about. Letting the gray find his own way along the narrow trail leading south and west, he closed his eyes and tested his surroundings with his other senses. The cool evening air caressed his cheeks, and the buzzing of insects and the rustle of leaves and the hoot of an owl were the only sounds. He sniffed the air, but the memory of the girl's scent filled his brain and blocked anything the night air might bring.

Eyes still closed, he felt the gray climbing, and he knew exactly where they were. He knew every inch of this country. This was his home. As the horse topped the little rise and dropped down the back side, there came a new sound. Distant hounds on the hunt. He opened his eyes. God bless you, Memaw. He burned to follow the sound, catch up to the hounds, be there when they caught the deputy. Though it wasn't black

Bowean, imagining this young deputy's screams filled his heart with longing. After all, this deputy consorted with Bowean just as if he were a white man.

With everything now easier, he kicked the gray into a trot. Memaw would be on the trail, for though she was past fifty and a mother and grandmother, she loved the hunt and could still run with the hounds better than most.

He stayed in the trees and circled Memaw's house and barn. Just as he expected, his brother's hounds were gone, and there was no one left to announce his arrival. He tied the gray behind the barn, crept to the back door, and eased it open. Tiptoeing, he passed Abe's bedroom, paused, and listened. Hearing nothing, he peeked in. Abe's bed was empty. Memaw was helping the boy become a man, just as she'd done for him. It seemed like a lifetime ago that she'd taken him out after the other deputy. His entire body tingled as he remembered the look on the man's face... and his screams.

He hurried down the hall, paused outside another door, this one with a long skeleton key in the lock. He pressed his ear to the door. Raspy, but rhythmic breathing vibrated from the room.

He pulled the door toward himself and turned the key ever so slowly until the bolt clicked. Holding his own breath, he listened until the breathing inside returned to its previous rhythm, then he opened his folding knife, turned the knob, and stepped into the room. His heart soared as he tiptoed to her side and clamped his hand over her mouth.

Her eyes flew open, and she pushed with her legs and slammed her head into the headboard.

He showed her the knife, then whispered, "Not a word."

Pressing the knife to her throat, he nodded to the door. "They're all gone, but you stay quiet just the same. Understand?"

She nodded.

The terror in her eyes filled him with longing. But they needed to get moving. Keeping the knife at her throat, he stepped to the window and unlatched it, then pushed her before him into the hallway where he relocked the door to the bedroom.

Outside, he unlatched the shutter on the bedroom window.

As they rode away, he pulled her close. She smelled of Memaw's salves and poultices, and her heart pounded in her chest.

*****

As much as he wanted to spend time with her, he opened a can of beans and set it on the table in the little cabin. "There's a chamber pot in the corner," he said. "I'll come back later."

She sat motionless on the bed, but he thought he saw a glint of fear in her eyes.

He smiled, blew out the lantern, pocketed the matches, and left, locking the door behind him. Outside, he re-checked the shutters, then hustled back to the waiting gray.

By the time he got back to O'Neal's old cabin, the morning showed the first hints of day. He needed to get into bed before the others awoke, but he took a minute to rub all the sweat from the gray, before turning him in with the other horses.

He took off his boots, shuffled across the floor, shucked off his shirt and trousers, and crawled into his bunk. His heart raced, but none of the others stirred. He closed his eyes, but sleep wouldn't come.

Minutes later, the sound of galloping horses woke the others. Ankor jumped up and peeked out the door. "It's Memaw and Abe."

Jared sat on the edge of his bed and mussed up his hair.

Memaw burst through the door. "Where is she?"

Jared rubbed his eyes. "Where's who?"

"Hannah. She's gone. Somebody light a lantern."

Jared feigned a yawn. "I suppose she'd just cut and run back to her folks."

The room lit up as Burg, dressed in nothing but a red union suit, struck a match on the table and touched it to the lantern.

Memaw's face looked red enough to burst into flames, and her narrow eyes burned into Jared. "She's in no shape to travel."

Jared shrugged his shoulders. "How would anyone get past the dogs?"

"We was out tracking that deputy."

Jared raised one eyebrow. "You get him?"

She shook her head. "Looks like he fiddle-footed around back south, then hightailed it back to town when he heard us coming."

Jared grinned. "Smarter than most of his kind, but I wish you'd a caught him."

She sucked in a deep breath. "It's the girl he's after. If I found out you took her, I'll tan your hide."

Jared looked around the room. "We all been here all night, ain't that right boys?"

The men all nodded.

Jared stood up and stretched. "Abe, fetch a pail of water. Ankor get us a fire going, so Willy can feed our guests."

After they'd eaten, Abe pressed the back of his hand and yawned.

Memaw slid back her chair and stood. "Come on, Abe. Let's get you to bed." She turned to the four men still at the table. "Y'all stay right here. That deputy could circle back anytime. Everybody's watching for him, but he's cagey and I wouldn't put it past him to sneak back around."

All the men nodded.

She locked her eyes on Jared's and stared until he said, "Yes, ma'am. We're to stay here."

After Memaw and Abe left, the men played poker for matchsticks. But Jared's mind was elsewhere, and he'd soon lost his stake.

Burg, who'd had a good run, slid over a handful of matches. "Might as well keep playing. Nothing else to do."

"Nah," Jared said, sliding away from the table. He stood. "Think I'll go hunting."

"Hunting?" Willy said. "You heard Memaw. That deputy could still be around."

Jared's right hand flashed, and, in a blink, his cocked pistol pointed at Willy's head.

Willy thrust out his hands as if they could block a bullet. "I'm just saying."

Jared smiled. "I'm just funnin' with ya, but I hope that deputy is out there."

Burg set down his cards. "Fast draw won't do you no good against a Sharps."

He holstered. "I'll keep my eyes open."

Burg turned toward Ankor. "Go with him."

Jared puffed up. "I don't need no nurse maid."

"Not saying you do, but four eyes is better than two, and Memaw'll be fit to tie, if something happens to her baby."

Jared slammed on his hat and stomped toward the door. "Come on then."

Ankor looked at the rise behind the cabin. "Let's climb up there. Looks like we could find us a fat doe up there."

Jared shook his head. That's where I was yesterday. No deer sign at all."

They wandered around below the cabin, Ankor scouring every clearing for signs of a deputy or a deer, and Jared shuffling along, paying attention to nothing but his own thoughts. He would wait until they were all asleep again. He smiled. Memaw, she was just Momma then, had once told him that waiting made opening a gift all the sweeter. He hadn't believed her then, but he hoped it was true now.

They ate cold bacon and biscuits for lunch, then wandered west in a large circle that would eventually lead them back to the cabin.

Keekee, chuck chuck.

Ankor froze. The turkeys were close, maybe just over the next rise. He pointed his rifle, then pointed to his own head, then softened his knees and placed one foot in front of the other.

Jared pushed by and stomped over the hill. He'd kill a turkey, so they could head back to the cabin and take a nap. The turkeys flapped into the air. Jared drew and fired, then he fired again and again, and the turkeys were gone.

Ankor's eyes flickered between anger and confusion. "What was that?" He pointed to his head.

"I was telling you I'd make a head shot."

Jared spun on his heels. "I've had enough hunting. I'm going back."

At the cabin, he tossed and turned on his bunk, until sleep finally found him. It seemed he'd barely closed his eyes when a loud crack snapped him awake. He fumbled to pull his pistol from where it hung on the bedpost.

Crack! Crack!

Burg and Ankor laughed. "Go back to sleep. It's just Willy chopping wood for supper."

Jared dropped his feet to the floor and rubbed his burning eyes with his wrists.

"You feeling all right?" Burg asked. "You look like Hell warmed over."

"I'm fine!" Jared said as he tugged on his boots. He stomped out the door and past Willy. "It's getting so a fella can't take a nap around here."

Willy laughed. "If a fella slept at night, he wouldn't need to nap."

Jared stopped. "What's that supposed to mean?"

"You know what it means, cousin."

Jared glared. "What Memaw don't know, won't hurt her."

Willy shook his head. "I don't give two hoots about that picaninny, but you bring that deputy down on us, we're all gonna hang."

Jared narrowed his eyes and stepped close to Willy.

"You tell Memaw what I done; you won't need to worry about no hangman."

CHAPTER Twelve

Carson stopped at the edge of clearing beyond Herschel and Agnes's ranch. Far behind him, hounds still bayed. The three-quarter moon lit the meadow. The log cabin stood dark, but a tendril of smoke rose straight into the sky on the calm night.

The Texas cow ponies were gone, but that was a problem for another day. He skirted the ranch buildings, staying well out of rifle range, but he belted out an old cowboy song, in hopes the old couple would mark his passing.

When the door squeaked open, he squeezed the sorrel with his legs and galloped through the big gate and south on the trail to Rocky Comfort.

Once out of sight of the cabin, he turned back north.

He rode in the moonlight, pausing often to watch and listen. Well into the night, the baying stopped. Had they stopped hunting him or had the sound faded with distance? Either way, he had escaped. His shoulders dropped, and he took a deep breath.

He stopped at a small creek and chewed on a chunk of salty jerky, while the sorrel drank. He scratched the horse between the ears. "Sorry boy, looks like it's going to be a long night for both of us."

When the trees blocked the moon, he walked his horse and, when the light and terrain allowed, he trotted. He stayed to the east of the ridge that, judging by the smoke he'd seen the previous morning, formed the eastern boundary of the spread-out community of small farms.

When he felt he'd ridden far enough north, he tethered the sorrel at the base of the ridge, pulled his Winchester, and climbed up. From the few columns of smoke rising up toward the moon, he was still a half mile south and a half mile east of the first cabins.

He rode in as close as he dared to the first cabin and stopped near the old mule and the milk cow. Now he had his bearings. He peered into the darkness, trying to see into the barn to spot any horses that hadn't been there. This was going to be harder than he thought.

He had marked two more columns of smoke, thinking that would be all he could get to before the sun rose. He rode close to the first one. It stood on the north edge of a large clearing planted with wheat and corn. As he skirted the clearing, a white dog, the size of a small pony, bounded toward him, barking and growling.

His heart pounded as he pulled his pistol. The last thing he wanted was to shoot a dog, but the timber around the clearing was too dense to run and he couldn't let the dog hurt his sorrel. The dog stopped a few feet short and carried on his night-time concert.

Carson's heart thumped, and his hands tingled. He whispered, almost mouthing the words, "It's okay, boy. "It's all right."

"Brutus," a man shouted from the house.

The dog looked over his shoulder, then returned to his barking.

"Leave those coons alone."

Brutus ignored his master.

Carson kept moving.

Brutus accompanied him around the perimeter of the farm.

As far as he could tell, the girl wasn't here, but how could he be sure. He'd been a fool to think that he could see enough at night, even with the bright moonlight. He didn't even know which of the Texas cow ponies Crusher and his men rode.

He would check the next place, then head back to Rocky Comfort and try to raise a posse. That seemed the only way. But would they come out here and fight for a black child? He cupped one hand over his eyes and rubbed his temples. He would have to think of something on the way back to town. His heart sank. He'd failed again, and Hannah Green was probably, right this minute, paying for his weakness and lack of experience.

He wound through the trees and back up the ridge until he saw the third tendril of smoke. This cabin appeared to be well up the side of the ridge and at the edge of a string of hills stretching east and north. He checked the eastern horizon, then crossed the ridge, left the sorrel tied in a grove of trees, pulled his Winchester, and trotted over the crest and down through the forest toward the smoke.

As he neared, he eased into a walk and then to a

slow, one-step-at-a-time pace, testing each footstep before he put down his weight. For reasons he couldn't understand, he felt hopeful. Maybe it was the location. This cabin was set apart and didn't appear to be in a good location for crops or pasture.

He tucked the field glasses inside his jacket. He would be able to get close enough to this cabin not to need them. Stopping, he scanned the small clearing through the branches and leaves of a young oak tree. The cabin sat in a tiny clearing and backed onto the tree-covered ridge. A ten-foot-wide stream gurgled on the far side of the clearing. Five horses looked toward him from a small corral near the creek. The moon had set, and deep shadows made it impossible to make out the colors or markings, but the number was close.

He pushed a finger into his mouth and held it into the breeze, then eased back into the trees and circled back the way he'd come, before moving around and above the cabin to a point where he could see the door. From here, faint snoring whispered from the cabin. The wind now brushed his face, and the horses no longer looked his way. With the dense timber and brush behind him, he could wait for enough morning light to see the colors and markings on the horses and maybe even one or more of the men, and if it wasn't Jared Crusher and the rest of the horse thieves, he could steal back to his horse and ride back to town. As much as he hated to admit it, he wished Bowean was here to tell him what to do.

He fought to keep his eyes open until a line of morning sunlight hit the tops of the far western hill and crept across the valley toward him. As people lit their breakfast fires, tendrils of white smoke reached for the sky like bony fingers. There were many more cabins than he'd imagined. He counted eighteen, then quit when he realized that more and more appeared, and he'd lost track of which ones he'd already counted.

His stomach rumbled, and his bladder cried for relief. He should have thrown some hardtack and jerky in a pocket. Something to remember for next time. He kept his eyes locked on the cabin, backed himself a little further into the underbrush, unbuttoned his trousers and made water. He licked his dry lips and glanced toward the stream. With the line of daylight fast approaching, he shook his head and moved back to his watching place.

He settled in and listened as the night sounds, the last coyote howl, the distant bark of dogs protecting livestock, and the buzz of insects, changed to the morning songs of a million birds. A rooster's crow echoed from far across the valley.

Whoever was in the cabin was not in a hurry to start the day. Just as the light was about to hit the cabin, hoofbeats ripped him back to attention. He listened as a horse splashed through the stream.

Still deep in the shadows, someone rode up to the corral and unsaddled a horse.

Carson eased down the lever of his Yellowboy, but in the shadow of the hill, it was still too dark to even see the brass cartridge. He touched the cool, smooth brass and eased the action closed.

The man ripped up handfuls of grass and rubbed the horse before turning him into the corral. As the rider walked to the house, Carson squinted, but there was still too little light. The man appeared small and light, like Jared Crusher, but Carson needed to be sure.

He leaned against the tree and watched, while his Gatling gun heart beats slowed, and his breath returned to normal. He eased back and settled in to wait.

More hoofbeats! Again, his heart raced. This time, two horses splashed through the creek below the cabin.

Almost with the line of sunlight, a tall woman, long, gray hair flowing behind her, galloped up to the front of the cabin astride a big bay. Behind her the boy, Abe, he had seen at Nate and Elsie's cabin, followed on the same black pony he'd ridden before.

It looked more and more like these were his men. He remembered the mess that Ernie had made of things when Lijah Penne was holed up in a cabin, just like this. The Langston brothers had died that day.

Today, there was a woman and the boy and maybe Hannah Green to worry about. What to do? What to do? Nothing for now. Settle in and watch.

The cabin door opened, and the boy trotted to the stream and fetched a pail of water. Smoke from the chimney puffed white, then burned away, before settling into a steady white column.

Again, his stomach rumbled. That would be their cooking fire. He longed to sneak back to his horse. Even the thought of the stale hardtack in his saddlebag made his mouth water, but he didn't dare even creep over to the creek for a drink. Instead, he checked the loads in his Winchester and his pistols.

After less than an hour, the boy and the woman stepped out. Though the woman had gray, almost white hair, she stood tall and moved straight-backed and lithe, like a young woman. The boy carried a tin pail and tossed its yellow liquid contents around the corner of the cabin, then set the bucket back inside the door and ran after the woman.

Jared Crusher and three other men stepped out the door.

Carson raised the Yellowboy and settled the front sight on Jared Crusher's shoulder. He tightened his finger on the trigger, when one of the other men stepped between him and his prey. Carson hesitated. There was still the woman and the boy to think about.

Jared raised a hand. "See you soon, Memaw."

The woman turned toward him. "You mind what I said."

"Yes, ma'am. You know I will."

The woman shook her head and rode away as Jared turned back into the cabin, and Carson lowered his rifle.

The men remained in the house and the hours without sleep weighed on Carson like a heavy quilt. He pinched his own cheeks, shook his head, yawned, and stretched, and did everything short of propping his eyes open with twigs. Why weren't they coming out?

And then the door opened, snapping Carson back to full attention. Jared Crusher stepped into the clearing, followed by another man, carrying an old Enfield rifle. The second man turned and pointed toward where Carson sat nestled in the brush.

Carson froze, not even daring a blink.

Jared Crusher shook his head and marched off southwest into the scattered oak and hickory trees.

Carson listened to the rustle and crunch of the men moving through the trees. If he could capture these two away from the cabin, he could truss them up and go back for the others, but he would have to march them over the ridge to the sorrel, where he had a set of manacles and a stretch of rope.

He watched, catching glimpses of the men through the trees, until they had disappeared into a low spot. He rose to his feet and took one step when the door opened. Pushing back, he dropped into his hidey hole.

A tall, thin man, with dark hair and a blue shirt, stepped out and walked over to the horses.

Carson wracked his brain. Bowean had shown him posters on all the men associated to Jared Crusher and urged him to study them anytime he had a few minutes. He struggled to match the face to a name.

The man lifted a sack of corn and dumped out six piles for the five horses. He turned back toward the cabin and shouted, "Willy. We shoulda told Memaw to send Abe back with some more corn. These horses are gonna be hungry soon."

The man inside the house grunted a reply, Carson could not make out.

Burg. This one's name was Chick Burg. Wanted for robbing stagecoaches and rustling. Reward, a hundred dollars. Carson tried to see the poster in his mind. Other than Jared Crusher, who were his partners. Willy...? Willy..., Willy Norris, reward one hundred dollars.

Burg ambled up to each of the four saddles laying in the dirt beside the corral and untied the coil of rope from each one, then he leaned one foot on the bottom rail of the corral and watched the horses eat.

Not daring to leave, Carson settled in. Before long, the sun hit the hillside, and the day warmed. He sank even lower, and before he knew it, his chin hit his chest. He snapped open his eyes.

Burg had two of the cow ponies picketed in the small meadow and now stood in the corral, the remaining three horses circling at a lope. He stepped forward, and the horses stopped. He flipped an overhand loop. The rope arched toward the horses but dropped between two of them. He cursed and re-coiled the rope.

This time the loop settled around the neck of a well-built, grey cow pony. The horse pulled back for a flash, then licked his lips and walked toward the man. The man laughed. "You son of a gun. You're just playing. Best come on if you want some more breakfast."

Carson watched Burg catch the other two horses. Anytime he was sure the outlaw looked the opposite direction; he squirmed and pinched his cheeks.

Just as Burg picketed the last horse and headed toward the cabin, three shots rang out. Burg skidded to a stop and turned toward the shots.

A second man, Willy Norris, wearing a dirty, faded yellow shirt, appeared just outside the cabin door. "Boys must have found something."

Burg shook his head. "One shot, meat in the pot. Two, prolly won't do. Three, woe is me."

Willy laughed and nodded his balding head. "Guess it'll be side pork and beans tonight."

A few minutes later, Jared Crusher stomped back into the clearing, followed by the other man. The two men pushed into the cabin and slammed the door. First the men spoke, but the cabin walls muffled the words, then they broke into laughter. Finally, Jared

Crusher shouted, "To hell with you all. I got a lot on my mind."

Carson didn't know what to do. For some reason, his hunger had fled him, but his lower lip had cracked, and the babbling creek tortured him. He was about to sneak over for a drink when Jared Crusher stepped out and rolled and lit a cigarette. Soon Burg stepped out, and he and Crusher walked over to the corral and leaned on the top rail, talking and laughing and smoking and spitting.

Carson's thoughts had slowed from lack of sleep and hunger and thirst. Maybe he could cut these two out, then come back for the others. Should he?

With the slightest of motions, he shook his head. Though he'd seen neither hide nor hair of her, Hannah Green had to be in the cabin, and he couldn't risk taking the men, until he knew she was out of the line of fire.

He'd left the sorrel tied with no water. First chance he got, he'd back out of here. He hated to admit it, but he needed Bowean's advice.

CHAPTER Thirteen

The late afternoon sun bored into Carson's burning, sand-filled eyes. He'd allowed himself a few brief naps, but lack of sleep weighed heavy on him and though he sucked on a pebble, his mouth was almost devoid of moisture.

Jared left the cabin and dumped the last of the corn into one pile in the corral, then tossed the sack on the ground and stormed off.

The little gray pinned his ears, bared his teeth, and drove the other horses back. The line-backed dun hit the corral rails with a crash.

Burg burst from the cabin. "Hey now. Settle down."

Jared, standing near the creek, looked over his shoulder, then tossed another pebble into the water.

"You know better than that, Jared Crusher," Burg said. "All they're gonna do is fight, you feed them that way."

Jared spun around. "You want it done different, do it your own self."

Burg shook his head, climbed over the top rail, shooed the horse's back, and scooped up handfuls of grain and dropped them in different piles.

After he climbed out of the corral, the little gray chased the other horses from one pile to the next before settling on one pile of corn for himself and allowing the others to eat.

Burg walked over to where Jared threw rocks. "That's all the corn we've got."

Jared nodded his head and shrugged his shoulders. "Stake 'em out."

"We should keep them close at hand, in case the deputies come, and we have to run."

"Bea should have thought of that when she only packed one sack. Maybe you should have told her." He tossed the rest of the rocks in his hand into the water, spun around, and marched toward the cabin. "I'm going to tell Willy to get some supper cooking."

Jared disappeared into the cabin as Ankor stepped out.

*****

Carson needed to move in the worst way, but the late afternoon sun shone directly on his hiding spot and forced him to duck even lower into the shrubs that hid him and shade his eyes with his hand.

As the fourth man stepped out into the clearing, Burg raised his hands palms up and shrugged.

Ankor. The fourth man's name was Ankor Traynor. Worth fifty dollars.

Burg and Ankor paced around the clearing, waving their hands as they talked and smoked.

As the sun set, Willy poked his head out the door.

"Y'all come and eat."

Finally! Carson stood, but his numb legs buckled and forced him to stumble out into the open. He froze. After a few seconds, he turned and climbed the hill on pins and needles legs.

Something clattered to the ground outside the cabin.

Carson threw himself behind the nearest tree. He squatted low and peeked around. A tin plate, surrounded by reddish brown beans, lay in the yard, and Jared stomped toward the corral, his rifle in hand.

Burg stepped out. "Where you going?"

Jared kept walking. "I'll bring back corn." He picked up the rope laying beside his saddle, climbed into the corral and shook out a loop.

"Memaw won't like this."

"What Memaw don't know won't hurt her," Jared said as he tossed the loop onto the gray.

Willy stepped out and said something to Burg.

Burg shook his head, and they both turned back into the cabin and shut the door.

While Jared saddled, someone lit the lantern in the cabin and light streamed into the yard through the cracks around the door and shutters.

Carson looked left and right. Where could Jared be going? Carson glanced over his shoulder. There was no way he could make it to the sorrel, get back over the ridge and follow Jared, no matter where he went. He would stick to his plan and ride back to Rocky Comfort.

Once Jared splashed through the creek and disappeared, Carson turned and climbed back up the hill. He looked both ways and decided it would be easier, and though further, probably quicker to circle the rocky bluff to the north. He pushed himself until his breath came in gasps and his head spun. He needed to eat. On the east side of the bluff, he dropped into a small bowl. The creek that ran below gurgled and splashed not far off through the brush. He paused and looked and listened, then he eased through the undergrowth toward the water.

He dropped to his hands and knees and plunged his face into the cool stream. After a few gulps, he held in a mouthful and sat back on his heels, letting the cool sweet water soak into his dry cheeks and tongue. Across the creek in a tiny clearing, three piles of horse manure, still green and dark, sat on the ground. Carson's heart raced. He looked around but saw no movement in the deepening shadows. He listened but heard only the twitter of birds serenading the end of the day and the far distant crack of someone chopping wood.

He hopped onto a flat rock splitting the stream and leaped across to the far bank. The horse apples were cold, but smooth and damp. They'd been left since the last rains. A trail of broken twigs and faint footprints led east through the undergrowth.

He held a hand before his eyes and followed the path, stopping often to listen. He looked up to see a small cabin of neatly squared logs and a cypress shingle roof. Though the cabin looked to be in good repair, the brush and young trees growing around showed that no one had lived here in several years.

There was a bent steel spike pushed through a hasp on the outside of the door, and the wooden shutters were closed and fastened. Though someone had come here, they were gone now. He needed to tend to the sorrel and get to Rocky Comfort. As he passed the door, he rattled the spike in the hasp.

Someone inside the cabin gasped. Or so he thought. He glanced over his shoulder, then turned back to the door. "Someone in there?"

Nothing.

He pressed his ear to the door. Someone or something inside breathed heavily. "Who's in there?"

A high-pitched voice cried out. "Please don't hurt me."

Carson drew back the hammer on his Yellowboy, twisted the spike from the hasp, threw back the door, and followed his rifle into the cabin. With the shutters closed, the dim light through the door did little to illuminate the interior, and he ducked back outside and pressed himself against the wall.

"Who's in there," he said. "I won't hurt you."

No one replied, but someone breathed in the back corner.

Carson held the Winchester ready in one hand, like a long pistol, and fished a match from his pocket with the other.

He scratched the match against the rough rawhide wrapped around the stock of his rifle. The match flared. He squatted low and ducked back into the cabin.

A thin black girl cowered on a bunk against the far wall.

She thrust out a hand. "Please don't hurt me."

"Are you Hannah?"

She lowered her hand enough to see his face. "Hannah Green?"

Eyes wide, she said nothing.

"I know your brother, Thomas. I'm Deputy Marshall Carson Kettle. I'm here to help you."

The girl's eyes flashed when he mentioned Thomas's name, but she stayed pressed against the wall.

How did she get here? Had to be Jared Crusher. Carson's heart leaped. What if Crusher was on his way here now? He thrust out his hand as if to lead her away, but Hannah cowered as far into the corner as she could, her eyes wide with fear.

"I promise, I won't hurt you, but we need to go. Jared Crusher could be on his way here right now. Likely is." Her eyes flashed past his shoulder at the door.

He spun, but there was no one there.

She darted past him and out into the night.

"Wait! No!" he shouted. Then he sprinted after her.

She crashed north through the brush. She was running further from his horse. He ducked his head and churned his legs. He'd always been a good runner and with his longer stride, he soon ate away at her head start.

She gasped and thudded to the ground.

He spotted the fallen sapling she had tripped over, in time to stutter step and leap over it.

Hannah scrambled through the brush on her hands and knees.

He dropped the Yellowboy and dove onto his belly, catching one of her legs.

She kicked back with her other, hitting him square in the nose.

Tears sprung to his eyes, but he held the leg he had and wrapped up the other.

Her body softened, and a great sob burst from her. "Please let me go."

Carson held her legs and blinked back the tears, caused by the kick to his nose, from his own eyes. "I'm a Deputy US Marshall. I came out here to take you to your brother and your aunt and uncle. If you promise not to run, I'll show you my badge."

She looked back the way she'd come, then nodded.

He pulled the badge from his pocket and handed it to her.

She ran her thumb over the smooth metal. "Are my ma and pa...?"

Carson hesitated. Would she break down if he told her? She deserved to know. "Yes," he said. "I'm so sorry. Thomas and I buried them."

"Thomas is at Aunt Ruth's?"

"He is, and he wants me to take you there. Who locked you in the cabin?"

"Jared. Memaw was doctoring me. She said she'd keep me safe, but she left, and Jared stole me away."

"I've got a horse, but we need to get moving."

She nodded and climbed to her feet and took a step. Her leg gave way, and she almost hit her knees.

Carson stepped close. "Lean on me. We need to go, right now."

She put her arm around his shoulder, and they limped off into the night.

Every few minutes, Carson paused to listen.

"I don't hear anything," she said.

Carson touched her lips with his index finger. She jerked her head back but held her tongue.

Carson held his breath. Someone was whistling, and a horse pushed through the brush along the trail along the creek.

As long as the horse broke through the brush, the rider wouldn't hear them, as long as they moved carefully. He held a finger to his own lips and led her up the hill behind the cabin.

"Hannah?" Jared shouted. "Hannah, where are you? You come back here, girl. I brought some things for you."

Carson froze, then ducked them both behind a scrubby young pine.

Lantern light spilled onto the brush from the open door of the cabin, and pans and what could have been the bed being overturned, crashed as Jared ransacked the room. "Girl. You don't come back here right now, you'll be sorry."

Hannah gasped and her body trembled, then tensed.

Carson squeezed her shoulder and shook his head.

Jared Crusher appeared at the side of the cabin, and the light from his lantern lit the night, and the hillside, but not as high as the spot where Carson and Hannah stood, half-covered by the spindly pine tree.

Jared held the lantern at his waist and shuffled sideways through the brush to the back corner of the cabin. "Hannah! I mean it. You come back here right now!" He raised the lantern and looked behind the cabin.

The lantern light shone up the hill and reached them, though Jared's eyes were still scanning the brush behind the cabin.

Hannah gasped and tried to pull away from Carson.

Jared raised the lantern high. "I hear you up there. You can't get away."

Hannah pulled free and hobbled off up the hill.

Jared raised the lantern and pulled his pistol and

pointed it at Carson, now lit up by wavering lantern light.

At the same time, Carson raised the Yellowboy, but the rifle snagged in the pine branches.

Jared's pistol spewed fire, but whether from a rushed shot, or the bullet striking a branch, it struck a few feet to Carson's right.

Carson jerked the Yellowboy from the pine and aimed, but Jared had thrown himself behind a large rock, the lantern crashing to the ground and going out.

Carson fired a shot toward the rock, and the bullet ricocheted and sang off into the night. His first thought was to take the battle to Jared, then he thought of Hannah and fired one more shot before turning and ducking and diving up the hill after her.

Jared's bullets slammed all around him, but he never slowed and kept weaving through the trees.

When he caught up to Hannah, still limping and bobbing up the hill, and gasping in pain with each step, he grabbed her arm and flung her in behind a huge oak tree, then he peeked out the far side of the tree and flung two more shots down the hill.

"Leave the girl, and I'll let you live," Jared shouted. "I know every inch of this country. You won't get away."

CHAPTER Fourteen

Scattered pines covered the peak of the hill. Making things worse, the three-quarter moon began to rise and, before long, would light up the landscape.

Hannah fought gamely to keep up, but she gasped each time she put weight on her right foot, and tears streamed down her cheeks.

Carson figured they were no more than a mile from the sorrel. If they could get there before Jared caught them, they would make a run to Rocky Comfort. The sorrel would have to make the run without food and without a drink.

Carson ducked in behind a lightning struck pine trunk. Hannah tried to pull away and keep going, but he held on and whispered, "Just for a second."

She stopped and he kept one hand on her, leaned the Yellowboy against the rough bark, and cupped his hand to his ear. He heard nothing but his own and Hannah's heavy breathing.

He touched her chin and made her look at him

while he took and held a deep breath and touched his lips with his fingertips.

She nodded and touched her finger to her own lips and sucked in and held a breath.

He listened again. He couldn't hear Jared Crusher coming, but the night was quiet. Way too quiet.

They moved off again. As the moon rose higher, he tried to find low ground and clumps of brush that would hide them from pursuit coming over the hill. He recognized the grove of trees where he'd left the sorrel and made a beeline toward it. Almost there.

The sorrel must have caught wind of him, because the horse nickered his, I'm ready to eat and drink, call.

Carson breathed a sigh of relief when they got to the horse, and Jared was nowhere to be seen. He let the sorrel take a few mouthfuls of grass while he shoved the Yellowboy into its scabbard and tightened the cinch.

The sorrel shied away when Carson took Hannah's left leg and lifted her up from the wrong side. "Easy, boy. It's all right." Hannah hopped up against the horse on her left leg and stroked his big hip. Carson lifted again, and Hannah pulled herself tight against the back of the cantle of the saddle. Carson hustled around to the sorrel's left side and stepped into the stirrup. Hannah had to lean way back to allow him to mount.

Once in the saddle, he pulled out the Yellowboy and pushed the horse southwest toward Rocky Comfort. He breathed a sigh of relief. He would leave the girl with Bowean and come back for Jared Crusher and the others.

Just as he pushed the sorrel into a narrow trail through a thick grove of oak and hickory, Jared stepped the gray cow pony into the trail, his pistol out and aimed. "Stop right there."

Carson looked left and right. He burned to run, or fight, but the brush was so thick, he doubted the sorrel would go, and if he spun, Hannah might fall off or worse, get shot.

"Drop that rifle."

Carson set the Yellowboy, butt first, on the ground and let the barrel fall away.

"Now that hogleg," Jared said.

Hannah trembled behind him as Carson slipped the rawhide thong from the hammer of his Colt.

"Two fingers," Jared said. He licked his lips. "This bullet'd likely go right through you from here, and I don't want to shoot the picaninny."

Carson dropped the pistol into the dirt.

Jared laughed and shook his head. "You do stink, Deputy. I smelled you coming even before I heard your horse. You are the deputy that's been following us, ain't ya?"

Carson, seeing no reason to lie, nodded. "I am, so you'd best clear out of the trail and let me pass. If not, you'll bring the whole U.S. Marshal Service and likely the cavalry down on this valley."

Jared hesitated as if thinking, then he giggled. "They'll never find your body, deputy, so let them come. There'll be no proof. Won't find the girl's either." He looked past Carson. "You lift your head, girl."

Hannah pressed her face tighter to Carson's back.

"I said lift your head and look at me."

She trembled harder, yet she held her face where it was.

Jared rode up, keeping his pistol pointed at Carson.

He forced his fingers between the girl's chin and Carson's back and jerked until she faced him.

Carson eased his hand into the front pocket of his trousers. His fingers found the rounded grips of the Remington derringer that had ridden there since he'd taken it from Zeke's saddlebag.

"I said look at me, girl," Jared said. "I mean with those pretty brown eyes."

Carson leaned forward at the same time he pulled, cocked, and fired the little derringer in one motion.

Jared squeezed the trigger and fired his shot over Carson's back. The muzzle blast from Jared's Colt stunned Carson, but he fought through it and fired the second barrel as both horses leaped ahead.

Jared's gun arm caught Hannah across the chest and tore her from the saddle. The hammer of his Colt snagged in her dress and the pistol clattered to the ground beneath her.

Carson spun the sorrel and charged back toward Jared. Hannah scrambled out of the way.

Crusher stopped the gray cow pony, looked at his empty gun hand, down at the bloody bullet hole in the front of his shirt, then up at Carson. Blood bubbled from his lips as he choked out the words. "You had a sneak gun."

Carson nodded. "Used to belong to Zeke."

Jared held out his hand. "Give it to me. I'll give it to Bea. She'd want it." He slumped and tumbled to the ground.

Carson leaped down after him and knelt on his gun arm, before feeling for a heartbeat.

Jared stared up at the pale moon with vacant eyes.

Carson rose and rushed over to Hannah.

With wild eyes, she scrambled back.

"It's all right," Carson said, reaching out with one hand. "He's dead. He can't hurt you anymore."

She slumped, then pulled her knees to her chest and sobbed.

Carson wrapped his arms around the boney girl and held her until the sobbing slowed. "Come on. We need to get you to your brother and your aunt and uncle."

She wiped her nose on her sleeve and climbed to her feet.

Carson rolled Jared's body onto his shoulder and flopped him over his own saddle on the gray cow pony and lashed him on. He helped Hannah onto the sorrel and led both horses until they came to a little spring, he'd seen on his ride in.

After the sorrel had a good drink, he mounted in front of Hannah and loped toward Rocky Comfort.

Hannah sat stiffly, trying to hold herself on by gripping the rolled edge of the cantle. After a few moments, she wrapped her fingers in the sides of his shirt. Finally, she wrapped her arms around him and leaned her head against his shoulder.

The moon was straight overhead, by the time they hit the trail to Herschel and Agnes's ranch. Though it was unlikely anyone would be on the trail, Carson paused and watched and listened, before riding south and then taking the road west into the little town.

He pulled up in front of the sheriff's office, reached back and helped Hannah slide to the ground, dismounted, and tried the door. It was locked. He tapped on the door. "Bowean," he said in a low voice. Then he tapped a little louder.

Lantern light filled the dark office, and Deputy Bowean said, "That you, Kettle?"

"Let us in."

Bowean opened the door, and when the light hit Carson, glanced at the blood on his shoulder and said, "You hit?"

Carson shook his head and glanced back toward Jared's body. "It's his blood."

Bowean wrinkled his nose. "Skunk get you?"

Carson shook his head. "Mostly got my horse. I can't even smell it anymore."

Bowean grinned and waved a hand in front of his face, then he spotted Hannah pressed in close behind Carson. He held out his good arm. "You must be Hannah."

She nodded, stepped around Carson, and right up against the big black deputy. She looked up at his face, wrapped her arms around his middle, taking in his arm, still strapped to his chest, pressed her face to his shoulder, and cried.

He patted her back with his good hand. "You're safe now. Deputy Kettle brought you back. Now you dry those tears. Tomorrow, we're going to take you home." He turned to Carson. "You go get two rooms at the hotel and put this girl to bed, then take your horses to the livery. Leave the body there too. No use waking the grave digger tonight."

Carson nodded, but Hannah grabbed Bowean's arm. "I don't want to sleep alone. Can't I stay here?"

Bowean glanced at Carson, then back to the girl. "Here in the jailhouse?"

She nodded. "Is this where you sleep?"

Bowean smiled. "You'll have to sleep on the floor. Can't have you back there with that mean ol' Zeb."

She looked around with wide eyes.

"I've had plenty of sleep these past days. I'll stay

out here with you," Bowean said. He turned to Carson. "Go bring the blankets from that open cell. Bring the mattress too."

Carson did as he was told and stripped the mattress and the blankets from the bed Bowean had been using. He laid them on the floor against the wall and made a bed.

For the first time ever, Bowean thanked Carson, then he reached into his pocket and pulled out two gold half-eagles. "This is your share of what was left after I bought a good horse. You go on to the hotel. I'll stay here with Miss Hannah."

Hannah looked around the room. "Where will you sleep?"

Bowean patted his right arm, still wrapped against his chest. "I don't sleep much with this arm. "I'll just sit right there in that chair."

The morning sun streamed through the thin curtain over the window to the sparse hotel room where Carson slept. He had to climb the steep sides of the sunken mattress to get his feet on the floor. He washed himself with cold water from the blue enamel basin and a bar of rough, strong-smelling lye soap, then took a moment to stir up a little lather on the bar and cold shave the fuzz from his cheeks and chin.

He pulled his one change of clothes from his saddlebags and wrapped his dirty, skunk-smelling clothes in a bundle for the laundry.

He passed a cafe on his way to the jailhouse. The smell of coffee and ham and onions frying reminded him of how long it had been since he'd had a good meal and almost drew him in, but first he needed to check in with Bowean and see how Hannah had fared on her pallet on the floor.

Hannah sat across the desk from Bowean, her face drawn and weary. When Carson entered, she flashed him a shy smile, then turned her eyes back to the coffee in front of her.

Bowean looked up. "You get that body to the grave digger yet?"

Carson frowned, and anger swelled in his chest. "I've hardly eaten since I left here. I thought I might get breakfast before I did that."

Bowean shook his head. "Business before pleasure. You go find the undertaker, first. He can fetch the body himself."

Carson bit his lips and spun around. As he opened the door, Bowean said, "Once the sheriff gets here, Miss Hannah and I will join you at the cafe."

Carson gave the slightest nod and reached for the door latch.

"And don't forget to get a receipt."

*****

After breakfast, Carson leaned back in his chair and rested his hands on his full belly. "I was thinking, this afternoon, I could saddle the little gray for Hannah and take her to her aunts."

Bowean grinned. "That's what you get for doing your own thinking. There's still three men out there. Three horse-thieving, deputy shooting, wanted men. I'd go after them myself, but..." He looked down at his arm strapped to his chest. "I reckon even a cripple like me can get this pretty young lady to her aunt's house. You get some supplies and find those men."

An hour later, Carson pulled the sorrel from his stall at the livery.

The young man working there took his money and gave him a receipt. "Where you headed today, Mr. Deputy?"

Carson tightened his cinch. "There's always another crook to catch."

"You going after the other boys that were with Jared and Zeb?"

Carson slid his two rifles into their scabbards. "Like I said, there's lots of evil men out there."

"You reckon they'll hang old Zeb?"

"That'll be up to the judge at Fort Smith." Carson said. "My job's to catch 'em. It's up to the lawyers and the judge to cook 'em and clean 'em."

"You'd best be careful out in the valley. Jared and Zeb got a lot of kinfolk and friends out there."

Carson nodded.

A quick motion pulled his eyes to a dark corner of the stable. He dropped his hand and slid the thong from the hammer of his Colt. "Who's back there."

The hostler gave a forced chuckle, hesitated a beat, and said, "That's just my cousin Frankie. He's a little slow, but he helps out around here."

On his way out of town, Carson stopped in at the general store and picked up the food he had ordered on his way to the livery. He stuffed it into his saddlebags and headed east.

A hint of red dust hung in the air. Things were drying up.

CHAPTER Fifteen

Memaw sat at her big cypress wood table. She drummed the fingers of her left hand on the undulating surface, rubbed smooth by thousands of elbows, and serving dishes, and plates. A tan and brown fired-clay bowl filled with thick corn grits, stirred with butter and salt, grew cold before her, as did the mug of coffee near her right hand.

She glanced up at the old ornate wood, brass, and glass grandfather's clock on the wall, and her racing fingers slowed and picked up the tick tock beat. Tick. Tock. Tick. Tock. It was almost noon. Abe hadn't returned from O'Neal's cabin, and there was no sign of Jared or the black girl, Hannah.

She pushed back from the table and padded across the slick oak floor, her bare feet making almost no sound. Sliding into the soft leather shoes she always left by the front door, she stepped to the front edge of her broad porch, cupped her hand over her eyes, and stared off toward the trail that led south. Still no sign of Abe.

As she turned to go back inside, a faint plume of dust rising from the trail coming from the west caught her eye. She stepped inside the door, picked up the old double barrel 12 gauge that always stood in the corner of the entrance, checked the loads, and waited and watched.

Damn that Jared. He was her baby and for all the pain and grief and trouble he caused, he was her favorite. So much like his father, that sometimes when she saw him ride up, it was as if the old man had come back to life, but he hadn't, and he wouldn't, and Jared would never change. Sometimes she wondered if she should warn Bea of what she was getting into, but she supposed the girl had heard all the stories about the old man and was smart enough to figure things out for herself. She liked the girl. She was strong of body and mind. If anyone could handle Jared, she hoped Bea could. But of course, she knew from her own experience, the girl would fail to tame him.

The rising dust grew closer and closer until Cousin Frankie thundered into the yard. His dun horse dripped green-flecked white foam from the cheek pieces of his bit and sweat from between his front legs. Anger swelled in her. How many times did she have to talk to Frankie about sparing her horses? Then, seeing his face, her heartbeat raced. Why had he driven the palomino so hard? Were they already hanging Zeb?

As the horse broke down from a lope to a trot, Frankie leaped to the ground and stumbled to a stop at the edge of the porch. He struggled to speak. "They... Somebody... That deputy..."

She held out one hand. "Slow down. Is it Zeb?"

Frankie hesitated. "Well, yes. He's in the jailhouse, but..."

"Slow down. Are they going to hang him?"

"I don't know, but that young deputy killed Jared."

She grabbed her chest and sank to her knees on the rough porch boards. "Are you sure?"

Frankie nodded. "I saw him in the livery. Cousin Cy saw him too. The deputy covered him with a blanket, but I peeked, and it was Jared, and he sure was dead."

She dropped her thin backside onto her heels and her face into her hands. It always came to this. She thought she had accepted this as her life, but not Jared. Why Jared? Would the sadness never stop? The pain. Or would it just keep coming over and over and over? There was only one release, only one hint of relief—however brief—revenge.

She raised her head. Placed one foot on the porch, then pushed down on her knee with her old hands to help herself stand. She laid fierce eyes on Frankie. "You start gathering the men. When Abe gets back, I'll send him out to help you. We're going after that deputy, and any others that had a hand in this."

Frankie's eyes widened. "That's... That's..."

"Frankie! What?"

"The deputy's on his way here now."

Abe galloped into the yard from the south, followed by Burg, Willie, and Ankor. "Jared's gone. The boys figure he's got that picaninny and he's holed up with her somewhere."

Memaw waited until the boys stepped off their horses.

Abe met her eyes. "What's wrong, Memaw?"

She opened her arms. She knew how much Abe idolized and loved Jared. "Come here."

He stepped close, and she hugged him. Then she reached out one arm and beckoned for Cousin Frankie to join them. She hugged both young men, while Burg, Willie and Ankor looked on, their mouths hanging open. "Jared's dead. Frankie and Cy saw his body."

Abe jerked away. "No! Can't be."

Memaw nodded and said, "It's true. I felt it in my heart, even before Cousin Frankie told me." She took a deep breath. "Abe, I want you to go up on King's hill. Take Papaw's spyglass and watch for that deputy to ride past Agnes's. Take my old shotgun and you see him, you fire one barrel, then count to five and fire the other. Frankie, you go to Nate's first. Tell him he's in charge of getting everyone from around his place over here before that deputy gets into the valley. He gives you any trouble, you tell him if he don't hustle, he'll answer to me."

She turned her hard eyes on the other three men. "Y'all should have stopped him."

The three men looked at the ground. Burg glanced up. "I'm so sorry, Memaw. We did try."

Tears filled her eyes but had yet to spill onto her cheeks. "It's not your fault. I know how he was." She turned and saw Frankie standing with his hat in his hands. "Get going."

Frankie glanced at his horse, then at the house. "I ain't et yet."

Memaw frowned. "The rest of you split up and gather the men." She spun on her heels. "Come on." She led Cousin Frankie to the kitchen and handed him the cold grits.

He tasted a spoonful. "This is cold, Memaw."

She glared, and without her saying a word, he bolted down the food.

She took the bowl and spoon. "What are you going to tell Nate?"

"Gather the men, quick." He paused. "The deputy what killed Jared is coming."

She nodded. "Now git! And don't spare that horse."

*****

Carson turned north toward the little cabin where he'd found Hannah and the larger one where he'd seen the other three horse thieves.

He would leave the sorrel downwind and creep up to the edge of the trees. Once he was sure the men were there, he had a plan, and it didn't include calling them out the way Ernie had called out Lijah Penne, the day the Langston brothers died. He would wait until they were asleep, then he would shout out and tell them he had Jared Crusher and that he'd kill him if they didn't come out.

If they argued, or wanted to speak to Jared, he'd say he had him gagged, and he'd ask them how he would know Jared wasn't with them if he didn't have him.

Carson left his saddle and bridle on the sorrel but tied up the reins and tethered the gelding so he could graze.

He sneaked down the hill toward the cabin. Without getting too close, he shinnied up a tall oak, until he could grab a branch and step out onto a thick limb. His heart skipped a beat. The corral gate was open, and the horses were gone.

Now what? He climbed down to the lowest branch, hung from his arms, and dropped to the ground. He made a wide circle through the trees until he got close enough to see that someone had bolted the door shut with a spike similar to the one, he'd found at the cabin above.

As much as he'd wracked his brain, he couldn't think of a plan to find the men. Maybe he could just wait here, and they'd come back, but what if they were gone for good? He dashed up to the cabin door, pulled the spike and glanced in. There was a table with four wooden chairs in the middle of the one room and a small cook stove against the back wall. Two bunks lined each side wall. One bunk had a bedroll, the other three just bare mattresses. He ducked back out, re-bolted the door, and hurried back to his horse.

One thing he knew, he had no friends in the valley, including Nate and his wife, but maybe he could still convince them to tell him where he might find Jared Crusher's men. He reached into his pocket and fingered the two gold coins Bowean had given him. Maybe he could buy some information.

If that didn't work, he would go back to his original plan of locating cabins, using the smoke from their cooking fires, and then sneaking in close enough to get a look at who was in each. It wasn't much of a plan, but what else could he do? It seemed everyone in the area was either related or friends, and none of them would likely talk to him.

By now, someone would be missing Jared, but no one would know he was dead, and Carson doubted word had spread across the whole valley. He turned the sorrel back the way he'd come in. He would circle back and instead of taking the main road, he would wind his way through the trees and come onto Nate's cabin from the east.

He would stick to his story and say he was down to his last few coins, but if they'd help him find Jared or any of the other boys with him, he would share what he had, and pay them more, once Jared paid him. He would say he remembered that Jared had called the other men Burg, Willy and Ankor. It wasn't the best plan. He didn't know what the boy on the black pony had told them, and he was almost sure the hounds had been on his trail the other night.

He rode on and pondered, and pondered, and rode on, until he saw Nate's cabin below him. There was no smoke rising from the chimney and nobody working the fields. The mule was gone from the pasture, and Carson suspected they weren't home.

He backed away from the crest of the hill, picketed the sorrel where he could graze, and settled in to watch.

After about an hour, Nate's wife stepped out of the house and into the yard and tossed some table scraps to the gray and white hens scratching in the dirt.

Carson decided to ride in. He didn't want to risk offending Nate by speaking to his wife when he was away, but he would stay on his horse and she could stay in the house. He would offer her ten dollars, a lot of money in these parts.

He circled the hill and came in on the same trail he'd used the last time. As he rode into the yard, she stepped onto the porch, brandishing the shotgun.

Her eyes shot open wide, then she took a deep breath and lowered her weapon. "Oh, it's you. You gave me a fright." She took one step back toward the door. "Nate's stepped away. He'll be back soon. If you want, you can water your horse, and wait in the shade. Wouldn't be proper for me to have you in, but I've got some pone and some venison, already cooked, if you're hungry."

Carson was hungry, but now was not the time. He tipped his hat. "That's a fine offer, but I still haven't found my friend Jared and I was hoping you fine folks could help me."

She shook her head. "Like I said when you was here before. I don't know no Jared."

Carson pulled a golden half-eagle from his pocket. "This is just about all I've got left. I really need to find Jared and get the rest of my stake so I can get going west."

Her eyes widened at the sight of the gold, and the shotgun bounced in her hands. "I bet if Nate thinks about it, he'll recollect where this Jared fella lives. Why don't you take care of your horse and I'll get you some lunch? While you're eating, I'll run and fetch Nate. He ain't too far away."

Carson dismounted at the water trough and let the sorrel drink, then he led him into the shade of a big, twisted oak, where the horse could pick at a little sparse grass, and Carson could see both the door, the trail he had just come on, and the path the boy had ridden in on.

Nate's wife, now wearing her bonnet, brought him a plate of cold venison and corn hoe cake.

Carson stood and touched the brim of his hat. "You didn't need to do that but thank you."

"It's cold, but it'll tide you until supper." She looked at the trail. "No sign of Nate. You rest here and I'll fetch him."

"Should I come with you?" Carson asked. "Then he wouldn't have to leave what he was doing."

She hesitated, shook her head and said, "The fella he's visiting is mighty leery of strangers. Best you rest here. I won't be long."

Carson nodded. "All right."

She trotted off, her bare feet raising puffs of red dust, and disappeared down the trail.

Carson slid the thong from the hammer of his Colt and settled down to his venison and pone. Though she'd brought him a fork, he set the corn hoe cake on top of the venison and ate it like a sandwich. His eyes flicked between the two trails leading into the clearing, and he listened for the sound of people or horses approaching.

After a few minutes, his attention drifted back to his thoughts. Was this a good move? Could he trust that Nate's wife didn't already know he was a deputy? He thought over her reaction to seeing him. The hair on his neck stood. He set the plate on the ground and rose to his feet. He glanced at both trails and peeked around back of the big, twisted oak. There was no one in sight and no sound of anyone approaching. Still, his fingertips tingled. He mounted, pulled his Yellowboy from its scabbard, and moved over to the shady side of the cabin.

After a few minutes, he dismounted and rubbed the sorrel's smooth, red neck. "This is crazy. She was more than likely just surprised to see me back." He slid his rifle back under the stirrup leather. "Come on. Let's see if you want another drink."

He glanced left and right, then walked toward the trough, kicking dust with the toes of his boots. His leather sole bumped something hard, and he reached down to pick up the nail he'd kicked from the dirt.

From the corner of his eye, he caught a flash of movement beyond the twisted oak tree. He picked up the nail and put it in his pocket. Without looking toward the movement, he stepped around the sorrel, putting the big horse between himself and whatever had caught his eye. It could have been nothing, but he thought it might have been a man wearing a faded red shirt. He made a show of picking up and checking the sorrel's right forefoot, then bent deeper and peeked under the horse's belly. Nothing big moved in the trees, and there was no red-shirted man in sight, but two gray squirrels squeaked out their syncopated alarm calls. Something in those trees had upset their afternoon.

CHAPTER Sixteen

Carson's heart raced. Had he seen a flash of red or not? If he had, he needed to put something other than his horse between himself and those trees. He backed the horse toward the cabin. The squirrels stopped their chatter, and he took a deep breath. Maybe it was nothing.

"Stop right there, Deputy," a man said from behind him.

Carson dove right and scrambled to the corner of the cabin.

A shot rang, and the sorrel spun, jerked the reins from Carson's hand, and darted off the other direction.

Carson rolled in behind the cabin and drew his pistol. He counted to three and peeked around the corner of the cabin.

A short, fat man, gray hair showing beneath his floppy brown hat, and wearing a faded red shirt and canvas trousers, darted across the trail Carson had ridden in on.

Carson slammed his back against the wall. Wild-eyed, he looked around for others. The sorrel stood prancing, head and tail high, across the clearing near the twisted oak. There was no safe way to get to him.

Carson had to figure out where the man had gone. "I'm no deputy. I'll come out if you promise not to shoot me."

"Come on out then, but don't let me see a gun in your hand."

The man was still somewhere near the trail.

"I'm coming out," Carson shouted, then he pushed away from the cabin and sprinted east toward the water trough, the creek, and the forest beyond. He hurdled the trough, then ducked left and back right.

A shot kicked up dust to his left and whistled off into the distance.

He darted one step right, then back left.

A second shot slammed into the dirt near the trees.

Without looking, he snapped a pistol shot back toward the man, and another, and then branches tore his hat from his head and he was in the trees.

He wanted to risk a look. Make sure there was only one man, for if there was, maybe he could outsmart him and get to the sorrel. Instead, he lowered his head and crashed through the undergrowth, putting as much distance as he could between himself and the cabin. Others would be coming.

He remembered the baying hounds, and he slowed. Without the sorrel and his rifles, they would run him down. He circled back and peeked out of the woods to see the old man, elbows flapping, galloping the sorrel along the trail the boy had ridden in on.

Memaw felt the blood boil from her heart up to her face. She had tatted the wee bonnet Nate's wife,

Elsie, had worn the first time her mother took her to church. Intricate lace flowers knotted together, and a white bow on one side.

How the mighty had fallen. When Elsie was born, her father, Dick, Memaw's own brother, had been top dog in these parts and Memaw had given the girl the hat she'd tatted for her own daughter, a daughter that never came. She smiled. Her own husband for all his weaknesses knew when to listen, and it wasn't too many years, of her whispering in his ear, before he ran the show in the valley, and now with the old man gone, she and her six, now down to three, strong sons had managed to hold on to power.

Now Elsie was a grown woman, she was disgusting. Just look at her standing in front of her father's run-down, once so beautiful house, and staring at her filthy feet.

Elsie's father sat on the threshold of the open door, his face so red, it glowed. "You got no call to talk to us like that. When I heared he killed Jared..., well, I saw red. Elsie thought I could take him, and I did too. Thought we'd save y'all the trouble."

Memaw stared until the old man met her eyes and quickly looked away. She turned to Elsie and spat on the ground between the man and his daughter. "How did that work out?"

Elsie held her eyes on her feet. The old man stammered and cleared his throat. "I got his horse. I got his rifles. Might have even winged him."

"See any blood?"

He shook his head and looked down. "He's afoot and all alone. He don't know this country. Mack's dogs'll have him treed before supper."

Memaw turned away at the sound of barking dogs

approaching. "You'd better hope so. He killed my Jared."

*****

Carson heard dogs barking in the distance. Not yet baying, they had yet to take up the hunt, but if he could hear them, they were too close. He scanned the terrain ahead. If he continued up and over the ridge, he would be heading toward Rocky Comfort, but he would never outrun the dogs. If he circled back, he might fool the men chasing him, but the dogs?

There had been a good-sized creek near the cabins. He'd heard a man could fool a dog if he could stay in the water long enough.

He sprinted until he could no longer gasp in enough air, then slowed his pace to a fast trot until he could breathe freely, then sprinted again. Staying in the trees, he forced himself through every patch of undergrowth he found, the denser the better. He wanted to make it hard for a man on horseback to follow and force those accompanying the dogs to do so on foot. He tried to push himself through a grove of blackberry bushes, thinking it would slow, maybe even stop the dogs, but the thorns dug into his skin and ripped and grabbed his clothes and forced him to back out.

He scrambled up a rocky bluff, paused, and tried to listen over his ragged breathing and pounding heart. Were the dogs baying? Were they on the hunt? He took in a deep breath and held it.

The dogs now bayed. They were on his trail.

He turned and sprinted down toward the cabin and the creek, skidded to a stop outside the cabin, tugged the spike from the door, and rushed inside. He snatched a tin can of pepper from the middle of the table and hustled back outside. The can was at least half full.

At the edge of the creek, he stopped and listened again, but the gurgling water blocked all other sounds.

He jumped out to the flat rock in the middle of the creek and hopped over to the other side. He ran upstream for a hundred yards, then stepped into the water and tried to run downstream on the slick flat stones. His right foot slid from beneath him and he plunged face-first into the water. He twisted as he fell, smashed his left elbow onto the rocks. Pain shot up his arm and through his shoulder, but he kept the pepper tin mostly dry. He slipped and slid and danced his way downstream past the cabin. He stopped and listened. His heart beat even faster. Even over the churning water, he could hear the dogs.

He plunged forward and splashed along for maybe a half mile, until he came to a short, steep, fast-flowing section. Here, the slick rocks and the grade forced him to slow down and carefully place each foot. At the bottom of the fast water, the stream took a sharp bend and flattened into a deep narrow channel. Huge old oak and hickory trees lined the muddy banks, and their branches reached over the water, forming a shimmering green arch, and stealing away much of the sunshine.

As Carson slid down the last slope, the bottom of the creek disappeared, and he plunged into his neck. He thrust the pepper can above his head, then gave up and tucked it into his shirt, so he could use both hands to swim through the slow-moving, dark water.

A big old snapping turtle dropped into the water

on his left, and another on his right. He pushed down a chest-tightening thought of snakes and focused on swimming as best he could, wearing all his clothes and his boots. As he swam away from the fast-moving water, he heard the dogs bay. They sounded far away, and he hoped they were heading upstream.

His arms and shoulders burned as he fought the weight of his sodden clothing and his gun belt. A cow trail pushed through the trees on his left, cut a deep furrow through the bank, and ended in a small wedge of sand pushing into the water. Maybe he should stop and strip off his clothes and gun belt before swimming on. He dragged himself to the shore, climbed onto the sand and gasped for breath. As his breathing stilled, the distant sound of the dogs cut through the trees. He still had some distance. Maybe it was time to leave the stream and circle back to see if he could find his horse and his rifles.

He dumped the water from his boots, then pulled the pepper can from his shirt and opened the top. Somehow, the lid had remained sealed and the pepper dry. He poured a tablespoonful into his hand and backed up the cow trail, sprinkling pepper as he went. He continued this way until, after about a hundred yards, he came to the edge of a large meadow, dotted with long-horned, red and white cattle.

There were no buildings and no one in sight, and he considered sprinting across the meadow and back into the forest on the other side. The baying sounded closer. He scattered the rest of the pepper, then stayed in the trees and circled the meadow.

He sprinted, ducking large branches, jumping deadfall, and plowing through the undergrowth. He wanted to get back near Nate's cabin and find his own horse, but with the dogs still coming, any horse would do. He would settle up with any owner when all this was finished.

The baying, though less frequent, sounded closer. How could the dogs follow him through the water? Did they swim? Did the water carry his scent? Wild-eyed, he looked the length of the long meadow. No dogs, but the relentless baying filled him with dread. Was this how hunted animals felt?

He skirted the end of the meadow and ran south through the trees.

"Git up," a voice shouted. "Git up!"

Carson skidded to a stop and eased to the edge of a large clearing.

A tall, thin, red-headed man pushed a plow into the red soil and shouted at an equally tall and thin, red mule.

The baying grew steadier and louder.

Carson dashed across the rough plowed field, pulling his Colt as he ran.

"Git up!" the man shouted, then he spun his head toward Carson, and his green eyes opened wide.

Carson pointed the pistol. "I'm Deputy Marshall Carson Kettle, and I'll be taking your mule."

The man shook his head. "No, sir. I need him."

Carson cocked the Colt, and the man raised his hands. "I'll try and leave him, but if I don't, you contact Marshal Greer in Fort Smith…"

The man shook his head. "No, sir. I need old Neddie."

Carson's shoulder hit the man's bony breastbone and drove him from his feet and flat on his back.

As Carson unhooked the single tree from the plow, the man fought to catch his breath. "No, sir. You can't take him," he said, rolling onto his belly and crawling up to his knees.

Carson had no time to argue and no way to convince the man. "Sorry about this, sir." He shoved the man with his foot and drove him back to the ground, turned to the mule, gathered the long driving reins in his hand, and swung onto the bony round back.

The baying dogs sounded ever closer.

Carson kicked the mule once, and the beast walked forward. A second kick brought a trot. He turned back to the man, now climbing to his feet.

"Marshal Greer. Fort Smith," Carson shouted over his shoulder. He gathered the reins into a long loop and whistled them through the air, whipping the mule, first on one flank and then the other.

The old animal arched his back.

Afraid the animal would buck, Carson squeezed with his knees, but the mule broke into a rough gallop, the singletree still linked to the trace chains, bouncing and rattling along behind.

They galloped along a narrow trail, then broke into a clearing with a cabin and a run-down barn. Three red-headed children, two young girls and a boy who was just walking, played in the shade of the cabin.

"Hey!" a woman shouted. "That's our mule." She sprinted for the cabin.

Carson leaned forward and thrashed the mule with the driving lines. He glanced over his shoulder.

The woman ran from the house and pointed a shotgun.

Carson pressed himself tight against the mule's neck.

Boom! Lead pellets stung Carson's backside. The

mule kicked up and tossed him onto the short mane on his neck. Carson scrambled to stay on as the mule found another level of speed.

Carson scrambled and pushed himself back, then touched the back pockets of his trousers. Thank God for distance. The pellets had stung him, but they hadn't pierced his thick pants. He sat up and tried to hear the dogs but the bouncing singletree and the rattling trace chains and pounding hooves and the old mule's wheezing, made hearing impossible.

Once they rode out of sight of the farm and the woman with the shotgun, Carson pulled the old mule to a stop. The animal felt as if he might collapse if they carried on, and Carson needed to figure out where the dogs were.

He slid to the ground and listened. He'd created some more distance, but the dogs still came ever onward. Keeping the lines in his hand, he unhooked the trace chains from the singletree and locked them to the hooks on the harness at the mule's hips. He pulled the knot holding the right driving rein to the bit, dropped the heavy leather rein, and tied the left rein in its place, leaving him with one, single, looped rein.

"Sorry, old boy," he said as he swung back onto the old beast.

The baying, now constant, drew closer and closer.

CHAPTER Seventeen

Carson stopped the mule short of the clearing around Nate's cabin, dismounted, and led the flagging beast to the edge of the woods. The gray and black hens scratched in the yard in front of the cabin; the old cow lay in the shade of the lone hickory in the pasture behind. Nate's mule was still nowhere to be seen, but most importantly, Carson's horse was not here.

He rubbed his tired eyes. The old red mule was running out of energy, the hounds still bayed behind him, and seemed to have boundless energy, and he was running out of options. He checked the loads in his pistol and counted the rounds in his belt. Twenty all together. Not much to fight a war.

He glanced at the cabin. Seeing no movement, he left the old mule tied to a sapling and sprinted across the yard. He leaned against the wall beside the door and knocked with the butt of his Colt. Nothing.

He knocked again. Still nothing. He unlatched the door and stepped through. Ned's shotgun leaned against the door frame. He picked it up, broke the action. Two unfired shells. He scanned the room. A box of shells sat on a shelf along the far wall. Eight more. He stuffed them into his pocket. Still not enough to fight a war, but more than he had a moment ago.

He picked up the shotgun and stepped out the door.

"You?" Nate's wife shouted from the mouth of the trail leading north.

Carson raised the shotgun, but the woman had already turned and run back the way she came.

"Stop," he shouted, but she kept going.

He lowered his head and sprinted after her, closing ground with every stride.

She glanced over her shoulder and seeing him closing, ducked into the trees.

He darted off the trail and cut a path that would intercept her if she continued the way she was going.

He stopped. Scanned the area. Where had she gone?

He listened and heard her heavy breathing, followed the sound, and found her huddled behind a thick blackberry bramble.

As he burst around the shrubs, she jumped to her feet, but before she got four strides, he was on her, and he shoved her to the ground. "Where's my horse?"

She looked up at him and hesitated as if thinking. "Did you really kill Jared?"

Carson nodded. "He left me no choice, but I haven't got time to talk. Where's my horse?"

"That's his brother Mack and his momma and a

whole passel of her lackeys follerin' those dogs. Your horse won't do you no good. They'll never stop."

"You let me worry about that." He nudged her with the shotgun barrel. "Where's my horse?"

She smiled. "Maybe you can thin her army a little. Come on. I'll show you."

At the edge of a large clearing, she stopped. "He's in the barn." She turned and shouted, "Pa. We're coming in. I'm with the deputy. Don't shoot us."

Carson grabbed her around the mouth with his left hand. "What are you doing?"

She pressed her face forward until he released her. "You want your horse?"

"You know I do."

"Then let me handle this. Them hounds are closing."

"I've got this shotgun at your back. Go ahead."

Her father, the old man that had shot at him at Nate's cabin, stepped out of the house with an old Enfield in his hands.

"Tell him to put down the rifle."

"Pa, put down the rifle. We're coming in and I've got an idea."

Her father set the Enfield against the wall. "Don't you hurt my girl."

Carson shouted, "Do what I say, and I won't, but I want my horse and my rifles."

The old man hesitated.

"Do it, Pa."

"Saddle the horse," Carson said. "And be quick."

The old man half ran, half hobbled to a run-down, big barn with a center two-story loft and a single-story wing on each side. Every second, the baying hounds drew closer.

Carson stopped in the yard and held the shotgun against the woman's back.

The old man led the sorrel out through the big double doors. "Now what?"

Carson bumped the woman with the barrel of the shotgun. "Now I take my horse and ride."

The woman said, "Jared's momma's name is Annabelle Crusher. She's got three boys left. Junior, Mack, and Gareth. She's the one ramrodding the stealing of all those horses outta Texas. But they're all part of it."

She turned. Hatred blazed from her eyes. "I want you to hang 'em all. Hang Burg and Ankor and Willie too." She turned toward the horse. "Or better, shoot 'em with that fancy buffalo gun you got there. That'd be best. Crushers is hard to catch and harder to kill."

The old man grinned and held out the reins. "Best light a shuck. Find a spot. Shoot them hounds of Mack's first."

"Take off your boots," the woman said. "Maybe your britches too."

Carson pushed by her and reached for his horse.

"You don't, they'll keep on you. I'll drag off your things and lead 'em all on a merry chase. I'll worry about those dogs, but you gotta decide right now."

"The dogs will catch you."

"They won't hurt me. Give me your things. Now!"

Carson kicked off his boots and pulled the derringer and the two gold coins from his pockets. He pulled down his trousers, leaving himself in his red union suit and his socks.

She turned to her father. "Gimme your belt."

The old man looked at her like she was crazy.

"Now!" she said.

He unknotted the cord holding up his pants and handed it to her.

While Carson tucked the little pistol and the coins into his saddlebag, re-buckled his gun belt, and swung onto the sorrel, she threaded the rope through the pull tabs on his boots and hung his trousers over the rope. He pulled the shells from the shotgun and tossed them one way and the gun the other, then he turned and galloped away. As he left the clearing, he glanced back.

The woman sprinted out of the yard to the east, his boots and trousers bouncing behind her.

As much as he wanted to stay and capture the men, Carson knew now was not the time. Between the dogs and the men, and at least one woman, hunting him, he couldn't win.

He galloped the sorrel along the main trail toward Herschel and Agnes's ranch and Rocky Comfort. 'For he who fights and runs away, lives to fight another day.' How many times had he bristled at his mother telling him this, yet now he saw the truth?

He would not, could not let this stand. He would return on his own terms and bring the murdering horse thieves to justice. Or maybe not. Now that he was a deputy, he was subject to orders from Marshal Greer, and he was already learning that sometimes Marshal Greer's priorities didn't mesh with his own.

For now, saving young Hannah Green would satisfy him. Besides, it appeared Jared Crusher was the worst of the bunch, and he was dead.

As he galloped up toward the rocky ridge, he stopped his horse. The dogs still bayed but sounded far away. Looking down at his red legs, he laughed, and wondered if Marshal Greer would reimburse him for his trousers and boots. He should have asked for a receipt. He turned the sorrel up the trail and pushed him into an easy jog.

At the highest point in the trail, a flash of movement caught his eye, and he dropped his hand to his pistol, and pulled and cocked it. A young man peeked over a waist-high rock, then ducked back down.

Carson drew the Colt. "I saw you there. No need to hide. I mean you no harm."

The boy stood, a brass spyglass in one hand and an old double barrel in the other.

It was the boy who had ridden to Nate's on the black pony. "You watching for me?"

The boy's face turned red, but he stood motionless.

"You tell them, that I left. Tell them I'm headed back to Fort Smith. Tell them they can give those dogs a rest."

The boy stared at Carson but made no indication he heard or understood.

"Did you hear me?"

The boy nodded.

Carson waved his Colt. "Easy like, I want you to pull the shells from that shotgun and toss them over here."

The boy's hands shook. He kept his eyes on Carson for several seconds. The boy's eyes showed both hatred and indecision. His lower lip trembled, like he was about to cry. He pushed the lever, broke the shotgun, plucked out the shells, and tossed them toward the sorrel's feet.

"What are you going to tell them?"

Tears welled in the boy's eyes and spilled onto his

cheeks. His eyes narrowed, and he choked back a sob and almost growled. "The deputy that killed Jared rode back to Rocky, and he's headed to Fort Smith."

Carson nodded. "Once I drop off this hill, you can gather those shells and ride on back."

He backed the horse until he had thirty yards to go to where the trail dropped over the rim and down toward the valley. As soon as he turned the sorrel, he heard the boy scrambling over the rocks.

He slammed his stockinged heels into the sorrel's sides and glanced back as the big horse took off.

The boy had picked up the shotgun shells and, with shaking hands, struggled to fit them into the weapon.

As Carson and the sorrel dropped over the rim, the boy fired the shotgun. Carson ducked, but nothing came near him. After a few seconds, the boy fired another shot. Carson hurried the sorrel down the steep slope and into the trees.

*****

Memaw rode her little yellow, pacing mule past Nate and Elsie's cabin. She'd ridden around the densest of the brush, keeping the baying hounds in earshot. She wanted to be there when they caught up with the young deputy. But even if she was a few minutes behind, they all knew enough to keep him alive for her.

Nate had run ahead with the other men and the dogs. Memaw rode close to the cabin door. "Elsie, you in there?"

No answer.

A distant shotgun blast sounded over the baying

hounds. She pulled the mule to a dead standstill. In the heat of the chase, she'd forgotten about young Abe, waiting and watching up on King's hill. Five seconds later, a second blast rang out. They were chasing the young deputy, so who was coming? An army of deputies? Bowean?

She pressed her heels to the mule and the little animal single-footed off down the trail. She whipped his flank with the end of the reins, and he broke from his smooth gait into a rough gallop.

She pulled out her Winchester and fired three quick shots into the air. By the time she reached Old Dick's rundown farm, the three floppy-eared tan and black hounds had been leashed and circled and bayed around her boy Mack.

"Call 'em off a minute." she shouted. "Abe signalled. Someone's coming."

"Wonder who it could be?" Mack, Memaw's short, thick, all-muscle son, said. "Dogs circled a might, but now they say the deputy cut back east."

Memaw frowned. "What's Dick say?"

Nate came out of the barn. "The deputy's horse ain't here."

"Where's Dick and Elsie?" Memaw asked.

Nate shrugged his shoulders. "They must have taken off somewhere on that big sorrel. Dick's team and Nate's mule are still in the barn."

Memaw turned to Mack. "Take Burg and Ankor and stay on the scent." She turned to the other four men. "Junior and Gareth, run ahead to the house and saddle four horses. Meet us on the trail to town. You other two come with me. I need to know who Abe saw."

Nate stopped. "I want to go with Mack. I'm

worried about Elsie. What if that deputy's dragging her along? Or worse?"

"Come on," Memaw said. "We'll worry about those two no accounts after we find out who's coming."

Nate sucked in a deep breath and looked like he wanted to argue.

Memaw met his eyes, and he dropped his head and started toward the trail.

As they drew closer to the trail to town, and the baying of the hounds faded, a cloud of dust showed over the trees. Memaw whipped the mule back into a gallop. "Come on, boys. We gotta get there first, see who's coming!"

Red-faced, Nate and Willy grumbled softly to each other, but broke from a trot to a flat-out run, trying to keep up with the galloping mule.

Memaw hit the trail first and slid to a stop. "Hold up!" she shouted.

Abe leaned back on his bridle reins and jerked his black pony from a hard gallop to a stop. The excited pony spun and danced.

"Who's coming?" Memaw asked.

Abe looked at her with a stunned look. The pony spun him away and then back toward her. "Why, nobody's coming. The deputy what killed Jared rode away."

Memaw's face turned purple. "Dick and Elsie!"

"No!" Nate said. "They wouldn't help him."

Memaw glared. "Where'd they go then? And how'd he get his horse? And who led them hounds off?"

"Please. They wouldn't..." Nate dropped his face into his hands.

"You'd best hope that deputy killed 'em quick, then."

CHAPTER Eighteen

People stared and pointed as Carson rode into Rocky Comfort wearing nothing below the waist but his stockings and his red union suit. He'd considered waiting until after dark, but decided talking to Bowean was more important, so he held his head high and rode right down the main street of the little town.

In one bow to what little pride he had left, he stopped at the hotel and picked up his laundered clothes.

The thin bespectacled desk clerk laughed as he walked through the doors. "Let me get your things. They're on the back step. Still a little skunky, I'm afraid."

Minutes later, Carson stepped into the sheriff's office. The sheriff sat on a chair near the cell, playing cards through the bars with Zeb.

Zeb's smile fled, and his lips narrowed to nothing. "I thought you'd be dead by now."

Carson smiled and shook his head. "Where's Bowean?"

The sheriff squeezed his cards together and pressed them to his chest. "Gone. Took the picaninny to her folks."

"He say when he'd be back?"

The sheriff's red face turned even redder. "Said he'd come straight back, and he was heading north whether you was here or not, then that uppity..." He took a deep breath. "He jammed his pistol right here under my chin and told me if I let Zeb go, he'd hang me in his place."

Carson chuckled. "I guess I'd be obliged to help, then. Marshal Greer told me Bowean's the boss on this trip."

Carson's stomach rumbled. "Let me get a bite to eat, and I'll come back and take over."

*****

The beef stew and biscuits disappeared in no time flat.

When the pretty red-haired waitress stepped from the kitchen, Carson was about to ask for seconds, but looking, he realized he was the last diner in the cafe. "How much do I owe you?"

"Two bits," she said.

He pulled a half eagle from his pocket. "Give me back nine fifty. Keep the other quarter for yourself."

Her face lit up, and her green eyes sparkled. "That's too much."

Carson laughed. "Probably not enough. I think my smell drove off the rest of your customers."

Her laugh brightened the room and his dark

thoughts. She grinned. "You do smell a little." She glanced back into the kitchen, then returned her eyes to his. "Could you eat a little more? It'll just go to waste, you don't"

He pushed his bowl toward her. "Yes, ma'am. I sure could."

In minutes, she set his full, steaming bowl on the table, along with a plate with four biscuits, and $9.75.

As he sopped up the last of the gravy with the last biscuit, she came out with a coffee pot in her hand.

He placed his hand over his cup. "I'd best let you get home."

She chuckled, and her green eyes lit up. "I am home. I live upstairs." She filled his cup, then pulled a second cup from behind her back. "Mind if I join you?"

Carson stood and pulled out a chair. "No, ma'am."

Her freckled cheeks flushed pink. "It's miss, Miss Ida Johnson."

"My name's Carson Kettle, Miss Johnson," he said, holding out his hand.

Her hand felt soft and warm in his, but the smile fled her eyes. "I know who you are, Deputy."

The touch of flutter fled from his chest. "Please. Sit down."

She sat and sipped at her coffee, then lifted her eyes and leaned across the table. "I don't know you, but you seem like a decent person, doing a hard job for someone so young. I can't imagine doing what you do, and I suppose you're about my age. Why do you do it?"

Carson rubbed the sides of his chin. "There's days I wonder that too. But bringing that girl back here and knowing that my partner has taken her back to people who love her, makes up for a lot of bad days."

"Is that why you became a deputy?"

He shook his head. "Was pure vengeance drove me to bring in my first man..."

She cocked her head and raised one eyebrow. "Did you make him pay?"

He nodded.

"Must have made you feel good."

He looked at the table. "Just kind of empty. Nothing could undo what he'd done, but it felt good to know he'd never hurt anyone again."

She smiled a weak smile. "You seem like a good man."

Carson shrugged. "I try to make my momma proud."

"Much as I'd like to get to know you better, you need to let Zebulon go, and you need to get out of Rocky Comfort. Get out of this whole country."

"I can't do that."

"Then, take Old Zeb and run as far and fast as you can."

Carson nodded. "Once my partner gets back, that's just what we'll do."

She touched the back of his hand. "Go now. And don't look back." She stood, gathered the dishes, and disappeared through the door to the kitchen.

Carson sat a moment, then rose, left a quarter on the table and walked out the door. Would he ever see Miss Ida Johnson again?

When Carson walked through the door, the sheriff still sat near the bars of the cell playing cards. He held his cards to his mouth and yawned, then reached out and took Zeb's cards and tucked them against the rest of the deck. "It's been a long day. I think I'll go home."

Zeb cleared his throat. "Ain't you forgetting something?"

The sheriff shook his head, reached into his pocket, pulled out two dimes, and handed them through the bars.

Zeb smiled, held the two dimes to his lips and pocketed them.

After the sheriff left, Carson picked up his saddlebags and sat in the chair behind the desk. He pulled out a small can of neatsfoot oil and a rag and a string and set to cleaning his weapons. He could feel his father's approval as he dropped the string down the barrel of his Yellowboy and pulled the oily rag through and watched it pop free, blacker than it had been going in.

He set his Colt on the desk, but before he unloaded it, he loaded the Yellowboy and set it, ready and aimed at the door, on the corner of the desk.

Though it hadn't been fired, by the time he'd cleaned and oiled his big Sharps, the sun was setting. He lit the lantern and settled in to wait. He yawned and rubbed his eyes. Tapped out a drumbeat on the desk. Picked up the deck of cards and set them back down. He pulled open the desk drawers one by one. Maybe the sheriff had a novel. Bowean should be back soon, then maybe he could take a turn on the cot in the empty cell before they headed to Fort Smith.

He got up, hefted the half-full coffee pot and touched the blue enamel side. He opened the door to the little stove. The fire had died down to almost nothing. He reached into the firebox with his hand.

Only the faintest hint of warmth rose from the gray ash. He twisted a sheet of newspaper from the kindling box, tied it into a knot, and set it on the coals in the firebox, then added kindling and finally a good-sized chunk of wood.

Once the fire blazed, he added a bigger chunk of wood and closed the stove door.

Before too long, steam rose from the pot and the smell of the strong, dark coffee filled the room. He poured himself a cup and was about to sit when Zeb said, "I'll have a cup, youngster."

Carson handed the cup, he'd just poured, through the bars.

Zeb touched his wrist.

Carson jerked back, spilling half the steaming coffee onto the cot, pushed up against the bars.

Zeb chuckled, "Didn't mean to give you a fright. I just want to talk."

Carson stepped back. "We got nothing to talk about. Let me fill this back up."

When Carson returned, he said, "Move back."

"I won't touch you again."

"Move back, or you'll get no coffee."

Zeb slid further down the bed and away from the bars.

Carson set the coffee on the floor and turned to go back to his seat.

"Get yourself a cup and come back," Zeb said. "I want to talk to you."

"I said, we've got nothing to talk about."

"I think you want to hear what I've got to say."

Carson filled his cup and turned toward the chair behind the desk. There was nothing Zeb could say that would make any difference. If he wanted to plead his case, he could do it before the judge in Fort Smith.

"I know who killed the last deputy that came into our country. Deputy's name was Delbert Butterworth. Disappeared from the face of the earth. Oh, how those deputies swarmed us. We had a few bad days and some of us took a beating, but Deputy Butterworth was just gone, never to appear again."

Carson paused just short of the seat of the chair.

"I know where they buried him and his horse, and them two picaninnies too. Helped dig that big old hole and cover it over, but I didn't kill none of them."

Deputy Butterworth was a legend. People around Fort Smith still talked about his disappearance. Carson had always assumed the deputy had disappeared somewhere in the Indian Territories, not here in Southwest Arkansas. People around Fort Smith said Butterworth was a hard man. Said it was a thin line between him and the criminals he brought in, more often than not over the saddle. But the deputies who'd worked with him told a story of a man fiercely loyal to his partners and tenacious on the trail.

Legend had it, he wasn't too careful or concerned about who got shot when he was after someone, that he figured you lie with dogs, you get fleas. And anyone anywhere around the outlaws he hunted had better watch out for themselves. He had many enemies, so no one was too surprised when he didn't return to Fort Smith. But everyone was baffled when the deputies came back without finding a single trace of the man.

For several years, Deputies had questioned every outlaw they brought in about Butterworth, all to no avail. Some folks speculated he'd done something so evil that he'd run off to hide his own guilt, but the deputies, who had worked beside him, knew better. In the end, even those who knew and respected the man moved on.

Carson walked back to the cell and slid the chair close to the bars. "Tell me."

Zeb laughed, then coughed and spit on the floor. "It's out in the valley. I'll have to show you. It ain't easy to find. 'Sides, you don't get something for nothing."

As much as Carson wanted to go, he had already stirred the hornet's nest in the valley and he wasn't keen to ride out there again, at least, not without a posse or a small army of deputies. Bowean would be back soon, and he would know what to do. "If you tell me, and I can find the body, I'll put in a good word with the judge."

Zeb shook his head. "Nope. You and me could ride out tonight and be there before morning. Once you're satisfied. You let me go."

Carson stood. "Do you know who killed him?"

Zeb turned and looked toward the small, barred window, then met Carson's eyes and nodded.

"Still alive?"

"Some are."

Carson knew that Deputies often let petty criminals go in exchange for information, but Zeb was involved in the murder of the Greens and Hannah's abduction, and that wasn't petty. But even in his short time with the marshals, Carson knew that Butterworth's disappearance was a scar that had never healed. "Would you testify as to who did it?"

Zeb shook his head. "That'd be a death sentence

for me. I might as well let you take me to Fort Smith. But there's some I know who might..., once you've arrested those that did it."

Carson stood. "Let me think on it." He reached to close the door between the office and the cell.

"Think quick. Bowean gets back here, deal's off. I won't deal with that circus monkey."

Carson paced from one side of the office to the other. Despite what he'd thought earlier about Bowean bossing him around, he wished the big deputy was there to tell him what to do. Or better, Marshal Greer. But Greer was sleeping in Fort Smith, and Bowean, though he should have made the trip and returned by now, was nowhere to be seen.

What had Captain Davis said back when Carson was hunting for Lijah Penne? Something about the cost of inaction being greater than the cost of making a mistake. But he'd also said a man had to think things through, then decide, and then act. If things didn't go as planned, and they seldom did, then think and act again.

He stepped toward the door to the cells, then turned and walked out into the dark street.

CHAPTER Nineteen

Carson slid one of the big doors open enough to let himself squeeze into the livery. The warmth and sweet smell of the horses rushed past him and out into the cool night. He leaned against the heavy door and shoved it all the way back to let the moonlight pour in.

Horses moved to the front of the long lines of stalls on either side of the stable and poked their heads into the alleyway to see what was going on. The sorrel nickered.

At the back corner of the livery, Carson rapped on the door of the tarped-in stall where the young hostler slept. Other than a snort and a slight pause in the gentle snoring, there was no reply. He knocked harder.

"What? What is it? Who's out there," the young hostler said.

"It's Deputy Kettle."

"What time is it?"

"Late."

A match scratched and flared, and lantern light brightened the canvas enclosing the stall/bedroom. "What do you want?"

"I want you to saddle my horse and Zeb's."

The young hostler opened the stall door and rubbed his eyes with the back of his hands. "Why so early?"

"Give them both a bait of corn. I'll be back in half an hour."

Twenty minutes later, Carson opened the door to the cell area.

Zeb looked up from his cot.

"Come on. We're going."

Zeb dropped his feet to the floor. "You got the horses?"

"The hostler's saddling them right now."

"You should have told me. What did you tell young Three?"

"Three?"

"The boy at the livery."

"Nothing. I just told him to saddle our horses. Why?"

Zeb hesitated. "No reason. I just don't want anyone to know I'm helping you."

Carson pulled the manacles and leg shackles from the corner.

"You won't need those," Zeb said. "As long as we've got a deal. I show you where Butterworth's buried, and you let me go."

"As long as I can be sure it's him."

"It's him."

"If we find his badge, I'll be sure."

Zeb scratched his chin. "What else you know about him?"

"Saw a tintype of him and Marshall Greer when they were deputies together. He was tall and rail thin, and he had a chin whisker long like a billy goat."

"He have that 10 gauge in the picture?"

Carson nodded. "He had a double-barreled coach gun. Looked like a Moore and Company."

"It's in the hole. I wanted to take it, but.... Never mind. It's in the ground with him if it ain't rusted away. He had the chin whiskers too. Could you see his hands?"

Carson shrugged. "I don't remember."

"Only had two fingers on his right hand."

Carson nodded. "I heard that." He stepped toward the cell.

"Before you unlock this cage, I wanna hear you say it."

"Once I'm sure it's him, I'll let you go. You have my word."

"Leave me here, while you bring the horses, and we're gonna need shovels."

A few minutes later, Carson tied the two horses behind the sheriff's office and trotted around to the front door. He paused on the step and looked west. The street was empty, and the only light came from the window of the saloon. He peered into the darkness beyond. Part of him prayed to see Bowean riding in, another hoped the big deputy was spending the night with Hannah's aunt and uncle. He hoped he was doing the right thing. He'd looked into Zeb's eyes and was almost sure the old outlaw was telling the truth. By all accounts, Butterworth and Marshal Greer had been thick as thieves. If he could bring in those who killed the deputy, Marshal Greer would have to let him work on his own... without Bowean. "Fortune favors the bold," he said to himself, as he opened the door.

*****

An hour later, they trotted along in the moonlight. Zeb led the way along faint trails that only someone long in the country would know.

Zeb pulled up. "Take these chains off. I don't like the way they clank and rattle."

"Nope," Carson said. "We get close to a cabin, you slow us up to a walk. How much further?"

Zeb cocked his head, hesitated, and looked all around. "Not far now. Another mile or so and we'll cross this ridge and drop into the valley. We'll be there 'fore first light. You bring a lantern?"

Carson shook his head.

"How you gonna see if it's Butterworth?" Zeb asked. He turned his horse and started back toward town. "I can't be seen with you."

Carson grabbed Zeb's Dun's reins. "I've got matches. If I can't be sure, we'll hole up until tonight." He hesitated. "I know where there's a lantern."

Zeb looked at him.

"The cabin where Jared hid young Hannah."

"What cabin's that?"

Carson shrugged. "It's tight built and tucked away in a little, overgrown hollow, about halfway up the other side of this ridge of hills."

Zeb thought a minute. "Tight-fitted corners, maybe fifteen foot by twelve."

Carson nodded.

Zeb turned his horse and rode on. He led them up

over the ridge and down the other side. About halfway to the valley floor, he stopped.

Carson rode close enough to whisper. "Is this the place?"

Zeb held his fingers to his lips and peered into the night. After a moment, he led them along a winding game trail and stopped beside the little cabin. "Get the lantern."

Carson smiled. Zeb couldn't trick him that easily. "We'll get it together." He unshackled Zeb's legs, then pulled his pistol. "Lead the way."

Once through the door, Carson lit a match. "Grab the lantern and let's go."

Zeb took the lantern from the table and stepped back outside. "Bring the shovels."

"Leave the horses?"

"It ain't far." He led north through thick brush, paused, then turned downhill and led them west. After a few minutes, he stopped in a small clearing.

"This it?" Carson asked.

Zeb nodded.

Carson reached for a match.

Zeb touched his hand. "Only when we need it." He turned and walked to a sunken patch of grassy ground about ten feet by six feet, then held out his hands to be un-manacled.

Carson shook his head. "You can dig with those on. You take that side and I'll stay here. And don't even think about using that shovel on me. I'll shoot you deader than yesterday."

After an hour spent cutting the sod and throwing dirt from his half of the big depression, Carson's hands and shoulders ached, and sweat covered his body. His shovel scraped off something firm and slick. "I think I found something."

From across the grave, Zeb said, "Light a match."

The flaring flame showed the dried and partially decomposed leather of a saddle.

Zeb stepped closer. "If I remember right, the deputy's buried against the horse's back and the piccaninnies down between its legs."

The match burned against Carson's fingers. He shook out the match, then lit another and touched it to the wick of the lantern. In the flickering light, he stepped forward and scrap the dirt from the area above the saddle.

A flash of movement caught his eye. He threw up his arms as Zeb struck down with his shovel.

Zeb's shovel slammed down the handle of Carson's and smashed into his hands, tearing his shovel from his grasp.

Zeb cocked back his shovel and swooshed the edge of the blade toward Carson's face.

Carson rolled as the edge of the shovel cut deep into the dirt. Driving with his legs, he scrambled back.

Zeb, his legs still shackled, lumbered toward him, then tripped and piled right onto Carson's chest, driving the air from him. Carson got one battered hand onto his Colt and fumbled at the thong over the hammer, while he used his other arm to hold the old man tight against his body.

Zeb twisted and tried to jerk himself free, then leaned forward and caught Carson's eyebrow in his teeth.

Carson fought to pull his pistol. The weapon hung in his clothing. He pressed down the grip, cocked, and pulled the trigger.

Boom!

Zeb grunted and his body jerked, then went limp.

Carson shoved the old man off and scrambled away.

Zeb rolled onto his back and up on one elbow and grinned from his perch in the hole. "I had to try."

Carson re-cocked the Colt. "I should kill you right now."

"Then you'll never know who killed Butterworth."

Carson held the pistol on Zeb. Something warm ran into his right eye. He touched his eyebrow and felt the torn skin. His fingers came away wet and red in the pale lantern light. "You bit me."

Zeb grinned. "Seemed like a good idea. Didn't work though. You still shot me. You wanna know who killed Butterworth, you'd best patch this hole in my leg."

Carson picked up the lantern.

Zeb's left thigh shone red and wet in the light.

"Crawl over to that tree."

Zeb rolled halfway over, then shook his head. "Cain't. Not without help."

Carson holstered his pistol and set the lantern on the ground. He grabbed the chain between Zeb's feet with his bruised and battered hands and drug the old man in a circle.

Zeb moaned. "Easy, boy."

Carson leaned back, squatted, and dragged the old man up and out of the hole. "Put your hands against that sapling."

Zeb pressed the manacle chain against the small oak tree.

"You try to fight or get away, I'll just shoot you."

"I ain't going nowhere. You don't fix my leg; you

might as well roll me into that hole with ol' Butterworth."

Carson pulled the key from his pocket, unlocked the bracelet from one of Zeb's hands, wrapped the chain around the tree and relocked it around Zeb's wrist. He pulled his knife and slit Zeb's bloody trousers.

The bullet had cut through the sinewy muscle of the old man's leg.

Zeb raised his head. "Leg ain't broke, is it?"

"Don't think so."

"Stop the bleeding."

"Tell me who killed Deputy Butterworth, or I'll let you bleed out."

"I tell you, I got no leverage."

"You don't tell me, you die."

"Our deal still good?"

Carson shook his head. "You broke our agreement when you swung that shovel."

"What if I say I'll testify as to who done the killing?"

"Did you see it?"

Zeb grimaced and nodded.

"All right, but you lie, or you don't testify, I'll charge you with attempted murder of a federal officer."

"Patch me up. If I live, I'll testify. I die, I'll come back and ha'nt you."

Carson used his own faded blue bandana and the bottom of Zeb's tattered canvas trouser leg to bind the wound. He turned to the hole they had scratched in the ground and Zeb's shovel still sticking out of the ground where Carson's head had been. "All right. Who killed him?"

Zeb moaned. "I'm sorry, my head's spinning."

"Who?"

"I don't recall. Maybe if you fetched me my canteen."

Carson pushed his shovel into the dirt and turned. "You're a good boy."

Carson strode over. Planted his boot heel on Zeb's bullet wound and pressed.

"Awwww!"

The old man squirmed and tried to pull his leg away.

Carson pressed harder until most of his weight rested on his heel.

"It was Jared's momma. Her and her boys."

"And you'll testify to that?"

Zeb hesitated.

Carson ground his heel against the wound.

"Yes. Yes! But you gotta promise you'll hang 'em all, else they'll make me pay."

CHAPTER Twenty

Carson scratched at the dirt with the shovel until a flash of yellow-white bone showed in the dim lantern light. He dropped to his knees and scratched with his fingertips, working his way down to what he thought was an arm bone. Tatters of skin, dry as old leather, came away as he brushed and blew on the soil.

He came to what looked to be a hand. He set the lantern close and used a twig to jiggle away flecks of soil until he uncovered the bones of two fingers.

Zeb had rolled onto his side and watched. "How many are there?"

"Two, as best I can tell."

"Told ya. It's Butterworth. I helped plant him myself."

Once Carson had cleared the outline of the body, he used the shovel to loosen the dirt and his aching hands to scoop it out.

He worked near the middle of the skeleton when his fingertips struck something hard, maybe a stone.

He dug deeper and scooped soil back and out of the hole. A gold watch still attached to a chain of gold nuggets plopped onto the ground near the lantern.

Zeb laughed. "Sometimes she's too cagey for her own good. If she'd a let me rifle his pocket, I'd a found that."

Carson pocketed the watch and scratched away a bit more dirt and found the rusty remnants of a coach gun, the wooden stock all but rotted away. He set it to one side and moved to the other side of the big grave. There he found, first a cinch ring, the mohair cinch and leather latigo long decayed to dust. A little further, he found two small skulls with patches of curly black hair still attached.

He dropped back onto his heels and thought of Hannah Green. What kind of people were these?

Zeb chuckled. "They was pert. Like house girls. Soft and smooth."

Carson glared, and Zeb shut his mouth. Carson's chest tightened until he almost couldn't breathe. Had he made a deal with the devil?

He leaned against the shovel. What more could he gain from digging here? He moved to where he guessed Deputy Butterworth's head might be and dug a half-inch at a time. If patches of the girl's hair remained, maybe some of Butterworth's had too.

He found no hair on the skull, only a neat hole just above where he imagined the ear to be, but he found long whiskers as he brushed the soil from the end of the jawbones. Bile rose bitter in his throat as he tugged the hairs from the bone and tucked them into his pocket.

The lantern flickered, and the flame faded as it consumed the last of the kerosene. He looked around. The eastern sky had begun to lighten. Zeb lay softly snoring.

Carson stood and shovelled the dirt back over the bodies. He'd let Marshal Greer decide if he wanted to come back and retrieve them.

The hole filled back in, he rolled Zeb with his foot.

The old man moaned, but his eyes flickered open. "What is it?"

"Time to go."

By the time they reached the cabin and their horses, sweat poured down Carson's face and burned in the bite mark over his eyebrow. Being a human crutch was hard work. Once he was sure the old man couldn't run, he unshackled Zeb's legs. Now he wondered how he would get him up on the horse.

"I want you to lean up against your horse, and I'll lift you by your good leg. Just lay over the saddle, and I'll help you get seated."

"Don't think I could stay in the saddle, even if you could get me up there. Leave me here with some water and food, and maybe a pistol."

"Nope. We'll get you mounted up there, and I'll lash you on."

Zeb grumbled, but moved in next to his horse and took hold of the saddle horn and the cantle.

Carson wrapped his arms around Zeb's good leg, dropped into a squat and heaved the old man up, until he lay across the saddle. The unwashed old man's smell filled his head. He held his breath for a moment, then said, "This might hurt a bit." He pulled Zeb's wounded leg over the dun's rump.

Zeb moaned, but pulled his body around and pushed himself upright in the saddle.

Carson lit a match and examined the rags covering

the wound. A tiny rivulet of fresh blood trickled down the pale, thin, hairy leg.

Carson used a leather thong from his saddlebag to lash Zeb to his saddle, then mounted and led the dun up and over the hill behind the cabin. The morning sun already lit the landscape on the east side of the hill. He would keep to the trees and low ground, and with any luck, have Zeb back in his cell before anyone spotted them.

They wound through the trees to the spot where Carson had killed Jared Crusher. A faint, distant scream broke the morning stillness. Carson stopped and listened. There it was again. Someone was hurting, or more correctly, being hurt. "What's over this hill?"

Zeb looked around. "Closest place would be Nate and Elsie's."

"I'm going to check it out," Carson said. "Do you want me to leave you on your horse or get you down?"

"I want you to let me go, like you said you would."

Carson shook his head and held up his battered hands. "Not until you testify."

"I told you who did it. I'll come to Fort Smith once you've arrested them."

Carson glanced at his battered hands and shook his head. "You're staying locked up until after the trial. Safest for you and safest for me."

*****

A few minutes later, dry grass tickled Carson's cheeks as he edged his way on his belly to the brow of the hill. Scream after scream and he was sure it was a woman. He crawled forward a few more feet and lifted his field glasses.

On the far side of the clearing, Elsie hung from her hands, tied high to a tree. Blood covered her bare back and her head hung to one side. A thick man with auburn hair handed a tawny, rawhide bullwhip to a straight-back, thin woman with a long, gray braid running down her back.

The old woman swung the whip back. Even from this distance, the whistling of the whip reached Carson's ears, then the crack of the thin rawhide on bloody flesh.

Elsie's body jerked and her head bobbed up as she screamed.

Two men held her father, one by each arm, and two more held Nate.

Why were they whipping her? A dog barked, and he knew. They'd trailed her and found out what she'd done to help him, and now they were making her pay.

Staying low, he pushed back. How much could she take? He had to do something. But what?

Once he was hidden by the crest of the hill, he ran back to his horse, shoved the Yellowboy into its saddle boot, then dug the box of big Sharps cartridges from his saddlebag, and jerked out the scoped rifle.

"What are you doing?" Zeb asked. "I can figure what's going on over there. You can't win. They'll run you down and when they do, they'll find me, and I'll get what she's getting and more."

Carson pulled the Yellowboy back out.

"You gotta take off these manacles or I can't use that."

Carson furrowed his brow. "This isn't for you." He

started back up the hill, then looked back over his shoulder. "You'd best pray I make it back. I don't, you'd better think up a good story, then start hollering."

Carson loaded the single-shot Sharps. He crawled back to the crest of the hill, set the Yellowboy to one side, and looked through the scope on the Sharps. Head hanging, Nate stood behind his wife. The gray-haired woman handed him the whip. He took it and let it drape behind him in the dirt. Elsie hung on her arms. Other than the occasional gasping breath, she didn't move.

The old woman pulled a pocket pistol from her dress pocket and pointed it at Nate's head.

He swung the whip and struck Elsie's back. She hung, limp and silent. Had she died?

The old woman cocked the little pistol.

Shaking his head, Nate swung the whip. This time, the whip whistled through the air and cracked against the bloody flesh.

Elsie screamed.

Carson froze. How could they do this? And how would he stop them?

The woman flicked the barrel of her pistol, and Nate again swung the whip.

Carson aimed for a patch of bare ground. He judged himself a half mile away. To come for him, they would have to cross the pasture and the bare hillside. If they were smart, they would run. If they weren't, he would be forced to make them pay with their lives.

Boom! The big rifle smashed back into his shoulder. The bullet hit the ground with a thud and a cloud of red dust. Everyone in the yard below, except Nate, scrambled for cover.

"This is the United States Deputy Marshals," Carson shouted. "Leave the woman and leave the area, or we'll arrest you all." A bullet smacked into the grass twenty yards below him. He ducked his head and rolled three times to his left.

CHAPTER Twenty-one

Carson peeked through the tall grass. The bullwhip lay in the red dirt. Nate stood beside Elsie, who still hung on the ends of her arms from the tree. He cradled her head and caressed her brow. The other men and the woman, including Elsie's father, had disappeared, but the three hounds bounced, barking and baying and ears flopping straight up the hill toward him.

Two men sprinted from behind the barn. Before he could find them in the scope, they disappeared into the trees to his left. Two more men burst from behind the henhouse into the trees to his right.

The dogs, white foam splashing from their jowls, had covered half the distance to him. Carson aimed at the lead dog, still coming way too fast, hesitated, then swung the rifle left. Chick Burg darted from behind a tall hickory and sprinted uphill to a thick oak. Carson held the scope on the oak, and when Burg darted up toward the next tree, squeezed the trigger. The big bullet tore through the man as if he were made of paper. Burg ran three strides as if nothing had happened, then threw up his hands and slammed face-first into the hillside.

Carson rolled back to where he'd started, pulled a big cartridge from his pocket, then dropped it and the Sharps and grabbed the Yellowboy. He fired a shot into the ground, just to the left of dogs.

The dogs veered to the right, away from the thud of the bullet splattering the dirt. Carson swung the rifle and fired two shots toward the men running up the hill to his right. Both shots missed, but the men threw themselves to the ground and fired toward him.

He snapped another shot to the left of the dogs, then grabbed the Sharps and shimmied back behind the lee of the hill. His heart pounded and metallic fear filled his mouth and nose. He wanted to mount the sorrel and run. He could easily outrun these men still on foot and even if they went for their horses, the lead he had and the excellent horses he and Zeb rode, would almost ensure he could get away. But no matter her reasons for helping him, he couldn't leave Elsie.

The dogs bayed and crested the hill. Carson didn't want to shoot them. He snapped another shot beside them and again drove them off their path, but they veered back toward him. Glancing at a huge old oak, he thought of climbing, but remembered all the animals his father's old hound dog had treed. He'd be trapped. He turned and sprinted down the hill, slammed the Sharps into its scabbard and swung onto the sorrel.

"Untie my horse!" Zeb said. "Can't leave me here."

The dogs were almost on them.

Carson spun the sorrel and galloped down the trail, kicking and ducking to avoid low branches.

The baying turned to barks.

"Git!" Zeb shouted. "Go on, Flop! He went thataway."

The dogs resumed baying.

Heart racing, Carson leaned lower over his horse's neck. The sorrel could outrun the dogs, but Carson couldn't run forever. He couldn't leave Elsie. A quarter mile along the trail, he turned the sorrel into a clearing that ran halfway up the hill.

He scanned the trees and brush at the top of the clearing and pushed his big horse toward the spot of thinnest growth. The sorrel slammed through the brush and bobbed and weaved around trees and rocks, changing leads every time he changed direction, as if in an agile, intricate dance.

Man and horse crested the hill and plunged down the grassy north face. Below lay the trail he had ridden the first time he'd visited Nate and Elsie's farm.

He hit the trail and pushed the sorrel for all he had. The sorrel approached the farm. Carson pulled his Yellowboy, and as the horse galloped into the clearing, stepped from the fast-moving animal, tried to run to keep his feet, but stumbled, slammed into the dirt, rolled, and came up with his rifle in hand.

Nate now sat beneath the tree with Elsie's head in his lap. There was no one else in sight and still the dogs bayed and came closer. Carson fought in a breath and trotted toward Nate and Elsie.

Nate saw him and wide-eyed, looked and pointed.

The gray-haired woman stepped from behind the corner of the house, a small five-shot pocket pistol pointing unwaveringly at Carson's head. "Nice of you to join us, Deputy. You'd best drop that rifle."

Though the woman was far away for the little pistol, her steady hand and unflinching gaze told Carson she knew how to shoot.

He hesitated. He still had his Colt and the derringer in his pocket, so he slowly set the Yellowboy on the ground.

The woman placed two fingers of her left hand to her lips and, without taking her eyes off Carson, whistled long and loud. "He's down here! Get back here and call off the dogs." She shook her little pistol and took a step forward. "Drop that Colt. Real careful like. I don't want to shoot you just yet, but I got this trigger half pulled, you don't do what I say."

Carson raised his right hand toward the butt of his pistol.

She motioned with the pistol, the tiny black hole in the barrel moving back and forth, like death's own eye. "Use your left hand."

Carson inched his left hand across his body toward the rawhide thong over the hammer of his Colt. He needed a distraction. Between the dogs and the men, he had little time.

"Hurry up, or I'll let the dogs have you for a bit before I have Mack call em off."

"Drop it, Annabelle," Elsie's father said, from the door of Nate's cabin, Nate's shotgun in his hand.

"You don't want to do this, Dick. He killed my Jared," the woman said.

"Oh, but I do. I been wanting to do this for years. It's time I took back what's mine. Now drop it!"

The woman shook her head. "Nope. He killed my Jared, and he's gonna pay. You shoot me if you're a mind, but my boys'll make you and yours pay." She took two long strides toward Carson. "Do what I say. Drop that Colt. Dick won't shoot me. He knows what'll happen to him and his girl and all the rest of his family if he does."

Elsie moaned.

Tears formed in Dick's eyes and the shotgun shook in his hands.

Carson held his eyes on the man and the shotgun, while he reached around with his left index finger and slid the thong from the hammer of his pistol.

Dick's trigger finger whitened.

Carson dove left and fumbled for his Colt.

BOOM!

The woman lurched forward and fired a shot into the space Carson had just vacated. Her eyes filled with rage. She took a half step around to her right, then teetered and toppled onto her side like a felled tree.

Carson pushed up to his feet and drew his Colt.

Four spots of blood appeared on the woman's back. Stunned, she rolled onto her hands and knees.

He sprinted three quick strides and stepped on her hand and the little pistol.

She tugged once, trying to free her wrist, then her sad eyes turned to Dick.

Smoking shotgun in hand, tears streamed down the old man's face.

Her sad eyes turned hard. "You shot me. Your own sister."

Dick wiped his left eye with the back of his hand. "Look what you did to my Elsie."

"She helped this murdering deputy escape."

"I never fought you when you stole my birthright. When you and that husband of yours pushed me from my rightful place. I should have been the leader here, but I let you have the glory. But this, this was too much."

She opened her mouth to speak, but all that came was bright, bubble-filled blood. She swiped at it with her left hand, then her face dropped into the dirt and her grip on the little pistol relaxed, just as the three dogs burst into the clearing.

Carson cocked his pistol and aimed at the leader.

"No!" Elsie shouted. "Flop! Heel!"

Just before Carson pulled the trigger, the big dog skidded to a stop, wagged his tail, and led the other two to Elsie. She pushed herself to a sitting position, reached out, and scratched the floppy black and tan ears. "I raised him."

A shot cracked and thwapped into old Dick's shoulder, slamming him to the ground. A second shot buzzed like an angry hornet past Caron's head. He ducked and dove behind the nearest big tree.

The thick-set auburn-haired man charged across the pasture, levering and firing his old Henry as he ran.

Carson glanced left, then right. Where were the other four men?

CHAPTER Twenty-two

Heart booming, Carson leaned against the rough bark of the big oak tree. Off to his right, Elsie screamed. "Poppa!"

Nate shouted, "Come on. We got to hide. They'll kill us all now."

"Poppa!"

Staying low, Carson ducked around the oak and snapped off a shot. His bullet hit just right of center and below the auburn-haired man's belt buckle.

The big man fired a shot into the trees as he spun and plunged to the ground.

Carson flew to his feet and dashed over to where Elsie had been tied.

As he ran, two men, one wearing a green shirt and the other a shirt of faded canvas, poked rifles from behind the henhouse and fired.

Carson threw himself behind the wide-trunked oak tree and squeezed in against Nate and Elsie and the three dogs.

Nate, eyes wild and wide, said, "We gotta run. They'll kill us all."

Elsie grabbed his arm. "We can't leave my poppa. He ain't dead, but he will be if we leave him. He shot Memaw."

Carson held his rifle barrel straight up, pushed with his legs, slid up the rough bark of the tree, popped out, and fired two shots, one toward each corner of the chicken coop. He pulled his Colt and offered it, butt-first, to Nate.

Nate just stared at the weapon.

Elsie winced as she reached up, took the Colt, and cocked it.

Carson's breath caught in his throat until she lowered the gun into her lap." I can't run, but I'll take who I can from here. I hear the others coming from beyond the cabin. Go! Kill them all!"

Carson handed his two-shot pocket gun to Nate.

This time the man took it.

Carson popped six rounds from the loops on his belt and dropped them on Elsie's dress. "Fire a couple of shots to keep their heads down."

She nodded and leaned out around the tree.

As she fired, Carson sprinted, bobbing and weaving through the trees. If he could make his way to the treed rise beyond the men, maybe he could come out of this mess alive.

A shot clipped a branch right behind him.

"He's trying to flank us," one of the men shouted from behind the chicken coop.

Carson snapped a shot back, ducked his head, and slammed right into a blackberry thicket. This time, there was no turning back. The thorns dug in, tore at his clothes, ripped the skin on his face, and tore hair from his head. He forced his hands and his rifle in front of his eyes and powered through.

As he broke into the open, blood poured from a slice above his eyebrows. A flash of motion, hazy and red through the blood, caught his eye.

The man in a green shirt snapped a shot at the same time Carson squeezed off a round.

The man's bullet tugged at Carson's shirt and burned his shoulder.

Carson's bullet hit the man in the breadbasket, doubling him over.

Carson dove for the cover of a fallen log, as the man fired two more wild shots.

The auburn-haired man in the yard was hit hard, but likely still alive. There was another man still somewhere near the henhouse, and this man was gutshot, but had crawled out of sight. And then there was Ankor and Willy, still coming from the north.

Think, think, think! It's still five to one.

A pistol cracked, and he chanced a peek. Elsie's father, Dick, knelt beside the dead woman, one hand on her gray head and his eyes turned to the trees. The auburn-haired man knelt a few yards behind the old man, his rifle pointed toward his head. Carson moved to shoot over the log, when the rifle slipped from the auburn-haired man's fingers and he tumbled to the ground.

Gun smoke floated past the tree where Elsie and Nate hid.

Four to one, and one of those hit hard and likely not long for this world.

Carson risked another peek. He needed to know where his enemies were. 'Better to fight and run away,' ran through his head, but he drove it off. Today he was through running.

"There's only three of you left. Throw down your weapons and move out into the clearing."

A shot thumped into the log.

Carson glanced over his shoulder, then rolled and wriggled in behind a hickory, just wide enough that he could stand behind it and be protected from gunfire.

A bullet hit the hickory.

The man behind the henhouse called out, "Burg. You and the boys get over here. I'll keep him pinned down until you can get around him."

"Sic 'em," Elsie shouted from behind her tree.

The dogs began to ki-yi and snarl.

"Call 'em off," a man shouted.

"Elsie. Call 'em off," a second man shouted.

"Drop them rifles!" Nate said.

"Heel!" Elsie shouted. "Flop. Heel!"

Suddenly, the clearing fell silent.

"Have you got your two?" Carson shouted.

"Yes, sir," Nate replied.

Carson cleared his throat. "You're all alone. Drop your rifle and step out into the open."

A bullet cracked into the tree.

Carson squatted and peeked.

The man in the canvas shirt sprinted into the trees beyond the henhouse.

"Keep those two there!" Carson shouted. "One of these two just took off north. I'll cut him off."

Carson swiped the rest of the blood from his eyes and sprinted after the fleeing man. After running a few yards, he stopped and listened.

Pounding boots and breaking branches grew ever distant.

Now what? If he went after the man, he could run into a trap. If he didn't, the man could circle back and ambush them, or worse, gather a small army and return.

He listened until the footfalls grew faint, then turned and ran back toward the clearing. He slowed and crept up to where the man in the green shirt had fallen. Spotting a patch of green, Carson pointed his Yellowboy and popped out from behind a tree. "Don't move."

The man lay motionless.

Carson eased closer. "Show me your hands."

The man did not respond. There was no rising and falling of the chest and no sound of breathing.

Keeping his rifle pointed, Carson rolled the man with his boot. The sticky, wet stench of torn guts filled his nose and throat, and he retched and gagged.

The man stared at the sky, his face as white as a flour sack.

Carson walked to the edge of the henhouse. "You all right over there, Nate?"

"We're fine. You?"

"The one in the green shirt's dead. The other one ran off."

Back torn and bloody, Elsie stumbled from behind the tree and dropped to the ground beside her father. "Poppa."

Her father pushed to his knees and cupped one hand over his eyes. "I'm all right, I guess. I killed her. My own sister. I let her do a lot of things to me over the years, but I couldn't abide what she did to you."

"Nate," Carson said. "Bring those two out here. I'll take them, then you can get Elsie and her father into the cabin and clean up those wounds."

Elsie looked up. "You all right, Deputy? You're covered in blood."

Carson dabbed at the cut on his forehead and brushed his fingers over the teeth marks in his eyebrow. "Just some scratches."

"What about your arm?" she asked.

He touched his shoulder where the bullet had cut through his shirt and the skin beneath it. "Just grazed me."

"We need to get out of here," Nate said. "Junior will be coming with help and we can't be here when he gets back."

Dick said, "Help me up and fetch me your shotgun and some shells. Junior'll have to learn who's in charge here."

CHAPTER Twenty-three

Trussed up, gagged, and secured to one of the posts holding up the crooked roof over the doorstep, Ankor and Willie sat back-to-back. Elsie waited just outside the cabin door, seated on a kitchen chair, close to the tied men. Her face tight and drawn, she sat with her spine poker straight, her battered, raw flesh not touching the ladder slats of the chair back. She fiddled with Mac's Henry rifle and held her eyes on the trail to her father's house and to Memaw's house beyond.

Elsie's father Dick leaned against the trunk of a big tree with a low fork that seemed made for shooting from cover. He held Nate's shotgun, and across the way, Nate leaned against a different tree and opened and closed the breech of the Springfield he held with the butt tucked under his arm.

Carson paced and swatted at the flies buzzing the wounds on his forehead and his shoulder. The waiting was the worst. If they were coming, let them come.

"Oh no," Elsie shouted. She winced and pushed herself from her chair. "No!"

"They coming?" Dick asked.

"Your house," she said.

Dick looked back at her. "Our house?"

She nodded. "Has to be. Or the barn. So much smoke."

Dick pushed back and around the tree and started down the trail at a hobbling trot.

Carson ran up and grabbed Dick's good shoulder. "That much smoke, it'll be too late. They're baiting you. They want us to come to them."

Dick's face reddened, and tears of rage welled in his eyes. "I can't let this stand."

Carson looked him in the eyes. "We stick with the plan. If you don't come to them. They're going to come to us." He picked up both of his rifles, the Yellowboy and the Sharps, and trotted away. He leaned both of his rifles on the big water trough, then reached in, scooped a handful of the brackish water, and rubbed it over the back of his neck. Hopefully, Dick would stay calm and convince Junior Crusher and his men that there had already been too much bloodshed.

"I see dust," Elsie shouted.

Dick waved toward the door. "Git inside. And keep your head down."

She stepped inside, but instead of hiding, she leaned against the door frame, the Henry in hand.

Dick stepped to the middle of the trail.

At first, Carson felt the hoofbeats on the ground, then he heard them draw ever closer until the man in the canvas shirt, Junior Crusher, led eight other armed men toward Nate and Elsie's cabin.

Fighting his wounded shoulder, Dick raised the shotgun and shouted. "That's far enough, Junior."

Junior slowed the big bay, then pulled his pistol and shouted, "Hee Ya!" as he spurred the horse straight at Dick.

The young man raced forward, cocking his pistol as he came.

"Don't have to be like this," Dick shouted, pointing the shotgun.

Junior raised his pistol to shoulder height and aimed at the older man.

Elsie shouted, "No!" and fired the Henry.

Junior's horse stutter stepped left, but Junior steered him back toward Dick. As he rode into pistol range, his eyes narrowed.

Elsie fired and missed again.

Carson's bullet slammed into the middle of the young man's chest and out his back in a spray of red.

Eyes wide and disbelieving, Junior fired a wild shot and slumped forward on his horse. The men behind him began shooting from their running horses.

Dick fired one barrel, then hustled back in behind the forked tree and pressed the shotgun through the V. At the distance he was at, the double aught pellets spread, striking two men and several of the horses.

The hit horses pitched and tried to spin around and run back the way they'd come.

Nate fired his Springfield, and Elsie fired again and again to no effect.

Carson found another rider with his front sight and was about to fire when Dick stepped from behind the tree and shouted, "Enough! There's been enough killing today. Stop this. Stop shooting." He lowered the shotgun, and to Carson's surprise, the remaining mounted men stopped shooting and fought their horses to an uneasy standstill.

Dick strode forward and dropped to his knees beside Junior, then reached down and closed the young man's eyes. He looked from the two wounded men on the ground and up to the mounted men. "Is this what you want? We're all kin, one way or another." He set his shotgun on the ground. "Kill me if you want to. I killed this boy and Annabelle. My own flesh and blood, so you want me, here I am, but you let my daughter and her husband be."

Carson kept his Yellowboy cocked and aimed.

One by one, the mounted men lowered their weapons and bowed their heads.

A tall, strong, black-haired man looked around the clearing. Pointing at Carson, he asked, "Is that who I think it is?"

Carson pushed his vest back to show his badge, and keeping the Yellowboy cocked and ready, stood. "I'm Deputy United States Marshal Carson Kettle."

The tall man raised his rifle and Carson raised his own and took up the slack in the trigger.

"You the one killed cousin Jared?"

Carson hesitated, wanting to find the right word. Not finding one, he nodded.

The tall man spit on the ground and turned to the five men still mounted on their horses. "Least we got someone we can make pay for all this."

The mounted men eased their horses apart.

Carson swung his rifle left and right.

"Oh, no you don't, Ben Crusher," Elsie shouted as she stumbled out of the cabin. She straightened her torn back. "There's been enough killing already today. We're gonna need time for burying and grieving, and if you kill this deputy, you'll throw us into another war. I hope y'all ain't already forgot the last time they came."

Ben Crusher met Elsie's eyes, then looked at his saddle horn.

Elsie took two more steps into the yard. "Get down off your horse and help Wilbur and Hardy into this cabin so I can see to those wounds." She turned. Her honey-rubbed, raw back shone red and angry past the bloody tatters of her dress as she hobbled through the door.

Ben slid his rifle beneath his stirrup and handed his reins to Dick. He turned to the other men still mounted. "You heard her. Let's get these boys inside."

Carson stood, but kept his hands on his rifle and his eyes on the men. He walked up to Dick. "I'll just take Ankor and Willy and be on my way."

Dick shook his head. "Even if I wanted to, I can't let you take them. The boys'll never stand for it."

Torn, Carson hesitated. It was his sworn duty to bring in wanted men, and he'd seen the paper on both Ankor and Willy. Besides, they, at very least, had been there when the Greens were murdered.

"Don't even think about it," Dick said. "I don't care two shakes of a lamb's tail about them two, but you won't make it out of here alive."

His mother's voice chanted over and over in his head. 'Better turn and run away and live to fight another day.' He nodded. "I need to know one thing."

Dick turned to him. "What's that?"

"Who killed Deputy Butterworth?"

Dick walked toward the cabin.

Carson needed to know if Zeb told the truth. He froze and watched Dick walk away.

Dick looked back. "Come on."

Carson followed.

As Dick passed Ankor and Willy, he stopped and looked at them. "You ain't going with the deputy, but the deputy's gonna ride out of here. Before I have Ben untie you, I need your word, you'll not try to harm him. Elsie's right. We don't need another war with the marshals."

Both tied men nodded and said, "Yes, sir."

Dick nodded to Ben and brushed through the men standing around the door.

Carson hesitated.

Dick turned his head. "Come on."

Carson turned his broad shoulders and did his best not to bump into the stiff and unyielding men standing around the door.

Inside, Elsie tended to the two wounded men, now sitting on chairs near the table.

Memaw, Annabelle Crusher, lay on the bed with her hands neatly folded over her chest.

Dick stepped close to the body and brushed a stray lock of gray hair from her brow. He tugged the gold chain around her neck and pulled out a crescent-shaped badge with a five-point star in the center. Most of the silver had worn away, showing the copper below. On the top of the crescent was the word 'MARSHAL', on the star, 'IT United States.'

Dick gently unclasped the chain and ran his thumb over the star. "Butterworth killed her man over a couple of piccaninnies he took. Annabelle and her boys killed Butterworth." He pointed northeast. "He's buried out in the hills. I could show you."

Carson held out his hand, and Dick set the badge and chain on his palm. Carson looked at the worn star and felt the weight of the heavy gold watch in his pocket. "That won't be necessary. At least not today."

CHAPTER Twenty-four

Carson rode into Rocky Comfort and tied his sorrel to the rail in front of the sheriff's office.

As he entered, Sheriff Cleve Moorman glanced up from the game of solitaire he had laid out on his desk. "Where's Zeb?"

"Gone."

The sheriff puffed up. "Dead?"

Carson wondered how much he could tell this man who was somehow attached to the people out in the valley, or at least feared them. "Nope. At least not last I saw him."

Gilmour Bowean, his right arm still bound to his chest, burst through the door. He slid to a stop. "What happened to you? You look like a tomcat's been at you." He glanced past Carson. "Where's Zeb? Did you let him get the jump on you? I was just getting ready to come after you."

Carson glanced at the sheriff and shook his head. "Let's talk outside."

Bowean sucked in a huge breath. "He'd better be dead, if you're back here."

Carson started for the door.

Bowean grabbed Carson's shoulder with his good hand and spun him halfway around.

Carson swung his arm and broke Bowean's grip on his shoulder, then stomped out the door. "I said outside."

Veins bulged like two lightning bolts down the center of Bowean's forehead as he stepped onto the boardwalk.

"Shut the door."

Bowean hesitated, then pulled the door closed.

"I let him go."

"You what?"

"He took me to Deputy Butterworth's grave and told me who killed him."

"And you believed him?"

"Dick O'Malley confirmed it."

"O'Malley confirmed it?"

Carson pulled the faded Marshal's badge from his pocket. "I got this from around Annabelle Crusher's neck."

Bowean squinted. "She dead?"

"Her and all her boys."

*****

Carson sat in the cafe with his back to the wall, watched Bowean step out the door, then wiped up the last of the sweet, reddish-brown bean juice with the last bite of the plate-sized steak he had just finished. He leaned back, watched the last of the supper crowd leave, sipped his coffee, and smiled. There would be plenty of time on the trail for boiled coffee and burnt bacon. Tonight, he had nowhere to go and nothing to do.

Miss Ida Johnson brought out a slice of cinnamon-smelling apple pie, a small pitcher of rich heavy cream, and the coffee pot. "Pie?"

Carson grinned. "Yes, ma'am..., I mean yes, Miss Johnson."

Her green eyes twinkled, and the dimple showed in her left cheek.

As he watched her walk back to the kitchen, a twinge of guilt swept through him. He hadn't thought of Ange in days.

Miss Ida Johnson stepped back out of the kitchen and set an empty mug, and a second piece of pie on the table. Her green eyes sparkled, and her cheeks seemed especially pink, as she topped up Carson's cup and then pointed to her own. "Do you mind if I join you?"

Carson didn't mind one bit, and he stood and pulled out a chair.

She filled her cup and sat. She narrowed her eyes. "Talk's all over town. They say some of the boys wanted to come in from the valley and do you harm. Kill you. But they say Old Dick's back in charge, and he forbade it. Say you treated them firm but fair."

"Good to know," Carson said. "Won't matter much longer. We're riding back to Fort Smith in the morning."

She stirred her coffee and then glanced up past her eyebrows. Her green eyes shone. "Folks don't like Sheriff Moorman."

Carson wondered where this was going. "Not my favorite either, I guess."

"Let's the boys from the valley run roughshod when they come to town."

"Shouldn't do that."

She placed her warm hand over his.

His heart skipped and beat double time.

"There's an election coming."

Where was this going?

"I bet if you stayed, they'd elect you."

"Me?"

She squeezed his hand. "There must be worse places to be than Rocky Comfort."

Hot blood flooded his cheeks. He shoveled in the last of his pie and burned his mouth as he swallowed his remaining coffee and set four bits on the table. "I'd best be on my way. My partner will need a hand.... He's got a broken arm."

*****

Hours later, Carson and Bowean slowed the horses to a walk, giving them a well-deserved breather. Both men rode in silence and had since leaving Rocky Comfort.

Bowean snapped from his own thoughts and looked at Carson. "What's that you say?"

Carson smiled and kicked his horse back into a trot and past Bowean. "Better to turn and run away and live to fight another day."

<<<<< >>>>>

Carson Kettle U.S. Marshal Book Three is available here: www.amazon.com/s?k=B08YXWYYNH

Afterward

March 14, 2021

I like to start these little afterwards with a heartfelt thankyou to everyone who reads my books, so please accept my gratitude.

I have a hard time expressing just how grateful I am to each and every one of you who trades hours of your most valuable resource, your time, to read my stories. I am honored and humbled by your support.

After our wonderful Christmas in Texas, we are back in the north country. We're still in the midst of Covid 19 restrictions, but life hasn't changed too much for me. I still write almost every day and I still throw hay over the fence to our livestock.

We had a mild winter, though it may not be 100% over yet. It's been shirtsleeve weather for our walks the last few afternoons. I try to get outside for at least a couple of hours every day. Spring is in the air. Our snowdrops are blooming furiously, and bees are buzzing the new blossoms. My old gray (now white) team roping horse, Snowman, is losing his winter hair in great white clumps, and our heifers are hanging out on south facing hillsides to nip at the year's first shoots of green grass.

As the seasons change, I find myself, more and more, longing for things to get back to normal. I want to travel freely and spend time with my friends and loved ones. This spring, our youngest daughter will compete in her last college rodeos. We planned to attend her last rodeo, which happens to be hosted by her own university, but the way travel is currently restricted between Canada and the US, it doesn't look promising. I guess compared to the losses and sacrifices of some others, my problems are minor, and we are truly blessed.

In my stories, Carson is learning that being a deputy marshal is at the same time rewarding and frustrating. In the next book, he's off to fight great evil and right more wrongs in the furthest reaches of the Indian Territory.

You can find all my books by clicking here to go to my Amazon Author Page.: https://www.amazon.com/Wyatt-Cochrane/e/B07JNZ79WD

If you would like to be notified of my new releases, please sign up on my website. I'll send you a free story when you sign up: www.wyattcochrane.com

Again, thank you for reading my stories and I wish you a wonderful 2021, or whatever year you are in if you read this later.

All the best,

Wyatt